W9-AYY-287

With thanks for your friendship and support.
Chuck Kocoras

by CHARLES P. KOCORAS

Foreword by
U.S. Magistrate Judge Jeffrey Cole

Where's Mine
by Charles P. Kocoras
© Copyright 2019

All Rights Reserved.

Published in the United States of America
in 2019 by Chicago's Books Press, an imprint of
Chicago's Neighborhoods, Inc.

First Edition, November, 2019

No part of this publication may be reproduced
or transmitted in any form or by any
means, electronic or mechanical, including
photocopy recording or any information or
storage retrieval system, without permission
in writing from Chicago's Neighborhoods, Inc.
or Charles P. Kocoras.

Errors or omissions will be corrected in
subsequent editions.

Edited by Jennifer Ebeling.
Produced by Charles P. Kocoras.
Designed by Sam Silvio, Silvio Design, Inc.
Printed in Canada by Friesens Corporation.

ISBN: 978-0-9961417-3-4
Library of Congress Control Number: 2019913265

To Grace,
Wife, Mother, Grandmother and Typist

And My Family,
For all that they give me.

ACKNOWLEDGMENTS

Although "Where's Mine" is based on Operation Greylord, a real and actual investigation conducted jointly by the United States Attorney's office and the Federal Bureau of Investigation office, both of which were based in Chicago, Illinois in the 1970s and 1980s, the incidents, events, characters and dialogue set forth in the book are entirely fictional and the product of the author's imagination.

The statistics cited in Chapter Thirty-One are true, however, as is the partial quotation of the Court of Appeals decision for the Seventh Circuit in finding the conduct of the Government lawyers and agents who participated in Operation Greylord honorable and lawful.

This book is dedicated to the many Assistant United States Attorneys and Special Agents of the Federal Bureau of Investigation who conceived, planned, and effectuated Operation Greylord. Although confronted with risks galore, including disclosures of their identities, physical harm by virtue of incarceration while acting undercover, loss of professional licenses, and being found in contempt of court for lying to judges, the overwhelming success achieved in Operation Greylord produced a system of justice in the courts of Cook County to which the citizens have always been entitled.

In particular, I wish to acknowledge the following persons for their particular contributions.

Tom Sullivan was the United States Attorney at the time the investigation was conceived. The courage he displayed in undertaking its implementation and the skill with which he supervised the conduct of his subordinates are deserving of the utmost respect and appreciation. Having once served as Tom's First Assistant United States Attorney, I can attest to Tom's courage and integrity in the discharge of the duties of the office.

Dan Reidy, an Assistant United States Attorney who would later become First Assistant U.S. Attorney, played the role of Chief

Operating Officer to Tom Sullivan's Chief Executive Officer's function. Overseeing the day-to-day events of the investigation and later personally prosecuting one of the most important judge defendants made the totality of Reidy's contributions extraordinary.

Terry Hake was an Assistant Cook County State's Attorney performing prosecutive functions while confronted with outcomes in criminal cases he believed to have been the product of corruption. Hake's moral outrage fed his professional discontent, and when the opportunity presented itself to be a key force in the eradication of the institutional misconduct, he seized it. Hake was instrumental to the broad success Operation Greylord achieved.

Dan Webb succeeded Tom Sullivan as the United States Attorney and inherited the Operation Greylord leadership role. Webb had started his legal career as an Assistant U.S. Attorney years before. It was in that early role that Webb established his incomparable work ethic and unmatched trial skills. When the two most important judge defendants' cases were set for trial, it was the unanimous decision of the office that Webb occupy the first chair at the Government's table in both cases. With those selections, the Government's chances for the return of guilty verdicts were enhanced. Both Cook County judges were convicted in their respective trials.

On a personal note, the contributions made by my wife **Grace** were vital. She typed the manuscript from my handwritings, including the revisions regularly made. But more than that were her constant words of support and encouragement.

Similar support came from my sons **Peter**, **John**, and **Paul**. Their belief in the worth of my work kept the project alive, even as my own faith in it flagged from time to time.

Magistrate Judge Jeff Cole is a longtime friend whose own written works are extraordinary in both quality and number. His support through the years has been steadfast, and I am grateful for his abiding friendship.

Judge Tom Durkin, my colleague on the District Court, volunteered to read a final draft of the book. His comments were both insightful and helpful and improved the final product. I am indebted to Tom for his contributions and his valued friendship.

Peter Vaira is a longtime friend who once served in the same prosecutor's office I did. Peter has also done a fair amount of writing and volunteered to read some early portions of my book draft. Peter also made suggestions to this novice fiction writer, which were much appreciated.

Jennifer Ebeling did an excellent job editing the book and I want to thank her for her dedication to this project.

Neal Samors has been a good friend for many years and I greatly appreciate his willingness to serve as publisher for this book and for working with me to promote and market it to a wide audience. ⚖

FOREWORD
by **U.S. Magistrate Judge Jeffrey Cole**

Five years ago Judge Charles Kocoras wrote an extraordinary book, entitled, *May It Please the Court:* A Story About One of America's Greatest Trial Lawyers." The book, which was about Dan Webb, quoted Brendan Sullivan of Williams and Connolly as saying: "There is only one Dan Webb in a generation. We all admire and respect him." A Review of the book then ended: "The same may be said of the author of '*May It Please The Court*.'" Given his exceptionally busy schedule and his commitments both in and outside the court, I did not expect that Judge Kocoras would have time for another book. Happily, I was mistaken, and we now have his second literary endeavor,"Where's Mine." The title, which was based on an old, not particularly flattering, Chicago proverb, could not be more fitting for a novel that explores the beginnings and evolution of what has come to be known as Operation Greylord—perhaps the most important, difficult, and successful undercover criminal investigation in the history of the United States.

Greylord was the shorthand name given to the investigation of what was thought to be—and which was confirmed by the investigation—the widespread corruption and illegality that was all too prevalent in the local courts in Cook County, Illinois, in both criminal and civil cases. The lengthy investigation revealed what was suspected: there was a core group of lawyers, who routinely paid off a core group of judges to secure favorable treatment for their clients. The pervasive dishonesty affected cases in traffic court, in the criminal courts and went even so far as to touch a number of judges hearing civil cases.

The passage of almost four decades has not lessened the importance of the Greylord investigation or the effect it had—and continues to have – on the public consciousness and the behavior of lawyers and judges not only in Cook County, but throughout the country. It is difficult to imagine that it has been almost 40 years since Operation

Greylord became etched in the public consciousness. Yet, it continues to have repercussions on the way lawyers and judges behave throughout the United States.

"Where's Mine" captivatingly tells the story from the beginnings of the investigation through the closing argument of one of the earliest and most successful of the prosecutions. But it tells it from a novelist's perspective and through the eyes of created characters. Throughout it all, there is authenticity in the deep feeling that one is witnessing the evolution of one of the Nations most important, undercover investigations through the eyes of those who actually participated in it. Of course, the protagonists are fictional. But there is the feeling and assurance of authenticity regarding how the investigation began, how it developed, and how it was consummated. The names of the players are fictional; the core of the story is not. We see the evolution of the entire case from the beginning. The thoughts and feelings and reactions of the *dramatis personae* are real and touching. From the outset there is excitement and personal involvement in all that is going on. You feel as though you are a participant in history—not merely a reader of it.

We are introduced early on to Saul Spencer, whose "pursuit of lofty goals befitting all of society" had given "way to the attainment of high fees from clients. Success in the courtroom was desired, not for its general value to the profession, but as a way to advertise for the retention of new clients and even larger fees. Idealism was replaced by mercantilism and, at some point, winning cases in whatever way possible ...." That was "all that really mattered." "A coating of sleaze [the author tells us] replaced the gloss of honor given to the nature of his practice."

We are spectators to the interactions between Spencer and his client, the infamous drug dealer, Mo Sands, in the unholy bond to bribe the judge in a case to get Sands off. Sands is told that $50,000 will "guarantee that you will walk out of here a free man." You won't be staring at 20+ years. After a good deal of back-and-forth Sands takes the deal. We are witness to the interaction between Spencer and Judge

Lunden, who takes the envelope quickly and immediately puts it in his briefcase." The ruling, of course, is in Sands favor. We are told it "must have set a record for brevity." And so begins the tragedy of Greylord.

We are witnesses to the beginnings and evolution of the Greylord investigation, in which the IRS would play such a pivotal role. We are taken into the inner confines of the meetings between the United States Attorney's office and the IRS Special Agent, that formed the underpinnings of Greylord. But the exploration of judicial corruption does not eclipse the vivid exploration of the lives and hopes and concerns of the Assistant United States Attorneys and the IRS Special Agents, who were so deeply involved in the investigation from the very beginning. Their lives, their hopes, their aspirations, their outlook on life and law are all explored from a novelist's perspective.

What makes this novel so special is that in passage after passage—page after page—it fairly rings with beautiful language and vivid imagery that the author uses to describe the thoughts and feelings of the book's characters, who are no less important than the investigation itself. For all those who believe they already know the story of Greylord, "Where's Mine" is a real eye-opener. Its characters, through whom the story is told, are multidimensional and sensitive. They come alive! And it is that character development that makes the book so rewarding. The reader already knows the ending. Yet, once you begin reading "Where's Mine", it's difficult to put down. The ending of the story becomes secondary to the thoughts and feelings and aspirations of those who are indispensable to the telling of the tale.

There are "transcripts" of various events that seem so real that one can hardly imagine they are part of a novel rather than part of real life. "Where's Mine" concludes with a fictional closing argument. It reads in part:

You have all seen, at some time or another, a statue of Lady Justice and the empty scales of justice before her, her eyes bound so that she cannot be influenced by the identities or interests of the parties before her. Her scales are empty of evidence and balanced evenly, awaiting only the quantity and quality of evidence to be put thereon so she can decide the case. Lady Justice represents the ideal – the way verdicts are to be arrived at, blind to the identity of the litigants and oblivious to any inequalities among them by virtue of their fortunes in life. Now that is the way you and I would visualize the Lady Justice depiction, blind to everything about the case other than its merits, determined by the weight of the evidence and the applicable law.

Thanks to the efforts of those who created and participated in Greylord, no longer is the outcome of a case a function of the old Chicago proverb, "what's in it for me?" No longer is the credo "where's mine" a factor in the decision of a case! Operation Greylord was simply the most successful undercover operation in the history of law enforcement, and it is told with great accuracy and equal sensitivity by Judge Kocoras. ⚖

Saul Spencer did not often take the time to interrupt the parade of his life and reflect on things past and present. It was never pleasant to do that, and satisfaction with how his professional life had developed was in short supply. His personal and family life was good, but that was about all that was. Although his attendance at law school took place over twenty years ago, it just didn't seem that long. Memories of his idealism about the law and its practice instilled in him the desire to excel in school. He dreamed that the lofty principles he studied in class and regularly debated with his classmates were but the prelude to an active law practice with more of the same.

Spencer never looked upon the legal profession as merely a way to make a good living and the riches many practitioners enjoyed. He knew if he was good he would always be able to put food on the table, but the inspiration which drove him was the majesty of the law as he saw it, and its necessity to an ordered society. Spencer believed lawyers championed notions of fairness and justice to all, and the system itself was predicated on the primacy of reason when evaluating the conduct of human affairs.

Somewhere along the way, the contributions to the development of the law he so strongly wished to make as a student and the high rhetoric of debate and discussion he regularly engaged in seemed to slip away from him. The pursuit of lofty goals befitting all of society gave way to the attainment of high fees from clients. Success in the courtroom was desired, not for its general value to the profession, but as a way to advertise for the retention of new clients and even larger fees. Idealism was replaced by mercantilism and, at some point, winning cases in whatever way possible and getting paid were all that really mattered. A coating of sleaze replaced the gloss of honor given to the nature of his practice.

One of the main reasons the buying and selling of illegal drugs continues virtually unabated in America and elsewhere is the money involved in its trade. There are no testing requirements to enter the business, and college degrees are not required. Because of their destructive consequences to people and societies, the penalties for those who are engaged in the business and get caught are substantial. For these reasons and others, great resources are devoted to their interdiction and to the prosecution of those who ply the drug trade. Naturally, lawyers who are experts in the defense of criminal drug charges and who enjoy success in court are able to command large fees. Saul Spencer had become one of those lawyers.

Saul Spencer was scheduled for an initial meeting with Moe Sands, an accused drug dealer. The meeting was scheduled to take place in the late afternoon in Spencer's office, a drab looking, poorly furnished office giving off a disheveled look with books and papers not always put away in an orderly place. Very little light came through the only window in the office. Spencer was seated at his desk and, although wearing a dress shirt and tie, the tie was loosened. Like the office, Spencer had a bit of a dog-eared look himself. Sands was seated in a chair off to the side of Spencer's desk. Contrary to Spencer's appearance, Sands, a stocky and handsome African-American, was wearing a gold bracelet around one wrist and a jeweled gold watch of prominent size and appearance on the other. Sands' shoes had been recently polished to a high gloss. He was wearing a pure white monogrammed shirt open at the neck, and a suit which looked rich and tailor-made. Sands was the epitome of style.

Spencer stood as Moe Sands entered the office and was seated. Spencer asked, "How ya doing?"

"I'm awright. Been better, been worse"

"Yeah, I know what you mean. The "G" can·be a mean dude."

"Yeah, especially when they make up shit to hang your ass."

"What do you mean?"

"I mean the case they're putting on me with my charge—the drugs, you know?"

"You mean that they planted the drugs on you?"

"No, man. I had the shit in my car, but they went and searched my car after that bullshit stop—they claimed I ran the light, but they must have had a snitch on me because they went right to the trap in the back of the car where the stuff was. It was only after they found it that they called in the dog who sniffed it and said to the prosecutors that the dog sniffed it out first and then they found it. That way, they justify a search they had no business conducting."

"How much did they find?"

"You know, man, that's why I'm here. They found two keys in there, and they're clanging the jail cell doors unless I cooperate and give them my supplier. And you know I got a sheet—two priors—and they told me I'm looking at ten for sure, and the top is outta sight."

"Yeah, I heard about the bind you're in."

"You got that right, and I'm told you're the only guy out here who can do me some good 'cause maybe you know the judge and he likes you."

"Well, I don't know about that, but I've had some luck with that judge. See, he's a stickler on the Constitution and all, and he's the one who decides whether it was a good search or a bad one. He's not afraid to pitch the case if the cops didn't do it right, no matter how much dope is involved."

"You mean, if I testify the way it really happened with the dog and all, bringing in the dog at the end, it's a bad search and I can walk?" "If that's how it happened, we got a real good shot at it, but you know, the cops aren't going to tell it that way."

"What'cha mean?"

"I mean they're going to say the dog sniffed the dope first and then they found the stuff, not the other way around."

"I know, but I'm telling you how it really went down and not the way they're going to tell it."

"That may be so, but then it's going to be who the judge believes— the way you tell it or the way they tell it. Was anybody else in the car with you?"

"No, but why does that matter?"

"Because there are two of them and only one of you. Besides, if you have to testify, they can bring up your two priors to argue that you are not believable and the cops are."

"Can they do that?"

"Yes. They can't use your convictions to say you dealt drugs before so it's more likely you were dealing them again, but the law lets the Government use those convictions and the judge can consider them in deciding who is more truthful, them or you."

"Well, what can I do? Cops lie, you know."

"I know that, and the judge knows that, but that issue has to be decided in this case and not what someone thinks may have happened in other cases. So it's one against two and the one-you-has some baggage."

"Well, what can I do? The prosecutors want to make a deal with me, but the main thing they want is my cooperation and you can believe if I have to testify against who I bought the dope from, me and the witness protection program will be together for life. Those boys play rough, and neither my life nor those of my family will matter at all to them. They'll be down in Mexico counting their money and I'll be visiting cities and towns I've never heard of for the rest of my life."

"I admit that it's a tough choice for you. But that's the game."

"Don't I have a shot with that Constitution-loving judge?"

"Yes, you do have a shot. He's a strong judge and if he believes your testimony, he's not afraid to pitch your case. And it won't hurt that I'm your lawyer."

'What do you mean by that?'"

"Well, I told you I have been in front of him before and I think he respects me. He has ruled in my client's favor in search and seizure cases, and I think he trusts me when I put on a case, even with a client like you."

"What do you think my chances are?"

"I can't say because I don't know how good the cops are going to be, but I think we definitely have a shot with this judge."

"I heard you were pretty tight with this judge, that he used to be a criminal defense lawyer and knew that cops don't always tell it like it was."

"I'm no friendlier with this judge than I am with any other judge, but, you're right, he used to be a criminal defense lawyer."

"Well, how would we go about defending the case?"

"What we can do is this: I can file a motion to suppress the evidence—the dope found in the car—and we'll have a hearing before the judge—not a jury. The judge will decide who to believe—you or the cops. If he believes you, he'll throw out the evidence and the case goes away. If we lose, you can decide at that time whether to take the government's deal—if it is still on the table—plead guilty and cooperate. It probably won't be too late to do that, although if the government thinks you testified falsely, they might look at you as damaged goods and their deal might not be as sweet as it could be."

"Tell me counselor, what would you do if you were in my place?" asked Sands.

"I can't tell you that; I can't decide for you. It is a highly personal decision. I've never been in jail before, so I don't know what that is like."

"I'll tell you what it's like—it's a motherfucker is what it is. And with two keys on the scale, it won't be pretty."

"I can't say you're wrong."

"Well, assuming we fight it at this point and challenge the search, what's it going to cost me to hire you?" asked Sands.

"I have to consider all of the possible outcomes, including an appeal if we don't win at the motion to suppress hearing. Although I think we have a decent shot at winning, I have to plan for all contingencies."

"How much you talking about?"

"Considering my chances of winning the hearing and my effort needed to do that, my fee for the whole package would be $150,000."

"Man, for that kind of money, you need to give me a guarantee that you're going to win. I mean, that's a lot of green!"

"I can't give you a guarantee—not possible. I can just tell you that I have had a similar case before and, luckily, before the same judge. I'm one for one, so the odds are in your favor. But no guarantees. Besides, those two keys you were going to sell—even at wholesale we're talking $40,000 to $50,000 and, at retail, well over my fee."

"You mean if we win, we can get the dope back?"

"No, we can't do that, but the weight and value play in to what's at stake in this case. It's like buying a Ferrari versus buying a Ford."

"You mean I'm the Ferrari or you're the Ferrari?" asked Sands.

" Put it this way. I'm the one driving the car and you have to pay for the ride you are going to get."

" Just remember, counselor, you better drive to the destination I want."

"Don't worry, I will." ⚖

Although a veteran judge, John Lunden was a recent appointee to one of Chicago's branch courts. The branch courts were located throughout the city of Chicago and County of Cook and were a part of the Circuit Court of Cook County. The cases handled in those courts were mainly criminal cases of all types, along with a smattering of civil cases. Their jurisdiction was based on geography, with boundary lines earmarking those cases which could be handled by the branch courts.

For judges assigned to sit in the branch courts, certain benefits were realized upon such assignments. One of those benefits was proximity to the judge's home and avoiding the necessity of going downtown to work with all the inconveniences such travel involved. Another advantage was the greater autonomy the branches afforded. The Chief Judge of the Court worked downtown, and rarely ventured out to the branch courts. Although each branch court had a presiding judge, a sense of camaraderie existed among the judges and staff as opposed to the more formal hierarchical structure which existed downtown.

The lawyers who practiced in branch courts were often regulars in particular courts, and friendships with court personnel and judges were not unusual. Although not a regular feature of life in the branch courts it was sometimes the case when a lawyer might drop in to a judge's chambers unannounced in order to exchange pleasantries. Such was the case one morning when Saul Spencer made his way to the chambers of Judge John Lunden. Nobody else was present. Spencer explained his presence.

"Good morning, Judge Lunden. I wanted to stop by and congratulate you on your appointment to this branch court. I happened to have a case up today, and I wanted to tell you how happy I am for you."

"Good morning to you as well," responded Judge Lunden. "It was a nice surprise for me to get promoted to a court with a variety of more interesting issues than the usual types of cases I've been hearing for the last few years. A lot of them were routine traffic matters, although there were times we had some interesting legal issues to deal with. If I'm not mistaken, I think you once had a tough search and seizure matter, the kind any judge likes to contend with. Besides the issues, I met a lot of nice lawyers through the years, guys who were pleasant to deal with, win or lose. Plus, the extra money the job pays with the promotion can always be put to good use."

"I'm happy to hear you are enjoying the work more and you have a terrific memory. I did have a couple of matters before you, and one of them involved an interesting Fourth Amendment search and seizure question. You really understood all the Constitutional principles involved and I was lucky to get you on the case. Maybe someday we'll have one that goes all the way up to the Supreme Court."

"Well, you never know. I remember my criminal law course in law school and how much I enjoyed the legal issues that we had to study. It was so interesting and I just loved it. Then I get my first assignment as a judge to traffic court, and I spend time listening to how many drinks a guy can consume before he gets tipsy but gets behind the wheel anyway. Most of the time nothing bad happens while the guy drives drunk, but every once in a while, he winds up hitting another car or, as you know from your own practice, killing someone. Tragic stuff. Although, in truth, the most serious traffic cases are the most interesting from a legal point of view."

"Well, that's in the past, so now you're onto bigger and better things. So tell me Judge, what does your call look like now—what kind of cases do you handle?"

"As you probably know if you practice here, we get everything. Lots of drug cases, assaults, batteries, thefts, some homicides—you name it, we get it."

"How does the assignment system work? I know you've got two full time judges here. How do you divvy up the cases?"

"The two of us just divide the days of the week; I handle the call on

Mondays and Wednesdays and Judge Bulger handles it on Tuesdays and Thursdays. Nobody sits on Fridays, so our assignments are based on what happens to be scheduled on the days we are assigned to sit. It works well that way and, over time, the workload evens up. Today is my day to sit, so I have to get out there pretty soon."

"Isn't that fortuitous? I have a case up today, and it involves a real interesting search and seizure question—the kind you say you like."

"What kind of case is it?"

"It's a pretty heavy drug case, but I don't think the car search that took place after a traffic stop is any good—at least that's our defense. But it's going to be a "he said, they said" kind of deal. Although there's a lot of dope involved, I've got a pretty decent guy who, if he goes down, is looking at a lot of time. He's got a couple of young kids and he's a terrific father. It would be tough on those kids if he went away for a long time."

"Have you tried to deal the case?"

"Yeah, there've been some discussions, but the prosecution thinks they have all the cards here and they're bargaining hard. He's willing to cop a plea, but they insist on cooperation. My guy thinks if he does that, he's looking at a different kind of sentence—death. That's a street sentence, but no less real. So he's between a rock and a hard place."

"I assume your fee is commensurate with the stakes in the case."

"No worries there. I'm covered for all contingencies. Whatever I need to, hopefully win, I've got."

"It sure sounds interesting. Is there a hearing scheduled?"

"Yes, I filed a motion to suppress the evidence from the car search, the state filed its denial, and we're all set to go. I'm pretty sure it's scheduled for next Monday, a week from today."

"It was nice of you to stop in and wish me well over here. As they say in our trade, I'll see you in court."

"It was good to see you, Judge, and I hope your stay here is even more successful for you than before. I'll see you in a week."

A hearing was held a week later on Spencer's Motion to Suppress Evidence. If Defendant Sands' motion was successful and the judge granted the motion, the state would be unable to offer the drugs found in Sands' car in evidence at the trial. A ruling in favor of Sands would effectively end the case.

At the end of the hearing, Judge Lunden stated in open court that he will take the case under advisement and would rule on the motion in one week. Immediately after the evidentiary hearing was concluded, Saul Spencer and Moe Sands went to Spencer's office.

Sands, in obvious agitation, no sooner sat down and asked Spencer, "Did you talk to that judge before the hearing? He didn't seem to be buying it. I mean, he did not look like he had a whole lot of sympathy or appreciation for my testimony or your argument. As for that goddamn dog, those dogs are so trained that they'll alert to practically anything that smells even a little bit, no matter when the dog is called in, before or after the search."

"Are you telling me that you committed perjury in there? That the cops were telling the truth about the dog alerting to the drugs before the drugs were discovered and seized?"

"What difference does it make when the dog was called in? It was going to sniff the drugs—or anything else—and alert to any odor it smelled."

"Look, it's one thing to rely on the law in your favor and the judge's friendship. It's another to put on false testimony in order to win."

"You mean, two legal sins are worse than one?" asked Sands incredulously.

"Look, we had a shot to win if what you said was true, but not if you lied."

"What are you going to do, counselor? Go and tell the judge your client is a liar besides a drug dealer, like you already told him I was. Or are you going to soak me with more fees and let it play out, and not risk your license by meeting with the judge alone prior to trial and discussing the case. What is it?"

"You got all the answers, don't you? Well, I'll tell you what I'm going to do. It's going to cost you another $50,000 to walk out of this whole deal. If you don't agree, I'm going to withdraw my appearance in the case. If I do that, the judge is going to know I'm defending a guilty man and your chances of winning are going to go down the drain. If I stay on, the judge will know that if he rules in our favor, he'll have a legally defensible—even courageous—position to defend if he suppresses the evidence and will be viewed as a hero in some circles. So what do you want to do?"

"Tell me, counselor, what's worse: a blackmailer or a drug dealer? Because I may be one, but you sure are the other."

"You can paint it any way you want, but I'm just trying to get all of us out of a bad situation. So, here's the deal. You pay me the $50,000 and I will guarantee you that you'll walk out of this a free man. You will not be staring at 20 plus years in jail without your family by your side and while those beautiful daughters of yours grow up to be beautiful, mature women. No acquittal and you get to keep your $50,000. Your family may need it."

"Why, you're as big a low life as I am. And how are you going to guarantee an acquittal?"

"You don't need to know that. If I don't get it, you keep your $50,000. If you walk, I keep the 50. And you need to give me the money within two days or it won't work. What do you say?"

"Here's what I say. I'm going to give you the money, you creep. But you better deliver because if you don't, I'll be getting more than my 50 back. I'll be getting what you fancy lawyers might call "revenge".

"Call it what you will. Every day you breathe free in the future, remember who put you on life support." ⚖

The very next day, Moe Sands returned to Saul Spencer's office carrying an oversized envelope. As he walked in to the office with Spencer sitting at his desk, Sands dropped the envelope on his desk. As it fell, it made a noticeable thud. Ignoring the usual pleasantry of saying good morning, Sands addressed Spencer.

"Counselor, you drive a mean bargain. I'm taking a chance on you pulling this off because if you don't, it's going to be a hard way to go for both of us. You know what I mean?"

Spencer looked startled and, indeed, a bit frightened. "Look, if that's a threat, we'll just call the whole thing off right now. I told you I can't guarantee any outcome and if it doesn't go our way, you get your money back."

Undaunted, Sands replied, "Counselor, I know you don't plan on giving me back all of the money I paid you, so you're going to make out real well, win or lose. I'm the one who's going to pay the price if you don't pull it off, and then I'll only have one thing to sell to the government if that happens. Know what I mean?"

"I know what you mean, but if you think you can trade me to the government in return for your freedom, you better think again."

Walking out the door, Sands replied, "I hope we don't have to see about that."

As soon as Sands left, Spencer's sense of bravado with which he delivered his final remark to Sands quickly disappeared. For the first time in his legal career, the thought of retirement made its way into Spencer's mind. Opening the envelope, Spencer's trembling hands counted out the $50,000 in cash. He put $25,000 of it in a legal manila folder and sealed it.

Having previously conducted surveillance of the courthouse, the parking lot with its assigned spaces for judges, and the normal time Judge Lunden left for the day, Spencer parked his car in a vacant space close to Judge Lunden's car.

It was late afternoon when Judge Lunden came to his car.

Approaching the judge after he got into his car, Spencer said to him, "Good afternoon Judge. Nice to see you again. I wanted to thank you for the way you conducted the hearing the other day. It was in keeping with the professional and scholarly way you always preside, and that's all anyone can ask of you." As Spencer handed the envelope to the judge, he said, "This is in appreciation for the fair hearing you gave us. My client and I know that, whatever the outcome, you will have done your best."

Saying "thank you," Judge Lunden took the envelope quickly and immediately put it into his briefcase. The following week, Judge Lunden issued a brief oral ruling granting Defendant Moe Sands' motion to suppress the drug evidence taken from his car on the grounds the search was illegal. The judge cited that his decision was based on, among other things, the credibility of the witnesses. The ruling must have set a record for brevity. ⚖

"What happens in Vegas stays in Vegas." This was an oft-whispered expression that promised secrecy for any and all of one's indulgences in the Sin City. You might think a prominent big-city, criminal defense lawyer would know that this Las Vegas hustle was not true, but some things just cannot be explained. Call it hubris, ego, or just plain "I don't give a damn," thousands of people a year simply pay no mind to the expression. Most probably do not pay a price for trusting the truth of it. Unfortunately for Floyd Siegel, he was not one of those who was unscathed for believing its promise.

Although the Big Brother of George Orwell's creation did not exist in the 1970s and 1980s, the federal government, in the form of the Internal Revenue Service, did have a toehold in the goings on in Las Vegas in those years. As an agency requiring the completion and submission of an endless variety of forms to it, the IRS managed to maintain an informational leverage on those who came to Las Vegas to gamble, party, and pursue their pleasures. They spent lots of money in doing so.

The form was called a CTR, Currency Transaction Report. It was a legal requirement that the casinos, hotels, and all other business establishments had to prepare a CTR when any of their patrons engaged in a currency transaction involving $10,000 or more. Although the currency level was high, the reach of the form's requirement was extensive. The form had to be prepared when a patron either received or spent currency in that amount. Not surprisingly, most of the people who had CTRs prepared for their transactions were ignorant of the form's submission to the IRS. There was no legal requirement that they be notified that such forms were required by the government and that their large transactions were being reported to the IRS. High rollers often knew about these tax regulations and sometimes structured their transactions in ways to defeat the reporting requirements. Many did not know of the requirements, however, or simply chose to ignore them in the way they operated.

Floyd Siegel was a man who did not know, or did not care, that IRS would be informed of any major currency transactions he was a party to. Winning big, losing big, or just spending big was simply his style of living, and altering any of his activities for reasons to keep information away from the IRS was something he was not prepared to think about. Siegel went to Las Vegas to have a good time and let his hair down in his personal pursuit of pleasure. To worry about the IRS and what it knew about him would take away from his good times, and he was not going to let that happen. That carefree attitude by Siegel would ultimately change his life.

It was early Monday morning in February 1977 when Assistant United States Attorney Dan Hogan was puttering around in his office. Being single and with no steady girlfriend, Hogan had no pressure to run out and get a Valentine's card for that special someone, because there wasn't one. He did not have any court calls that day, so his time was occupied with which of the six cases he had indicted and were pending in court might go to trial. All were in their early stages, so trial preparation for any of them was premature.

Hogan was awaiting the arrival of Ira Kessler, with whom he had made an appointment. Hogan had worked with Kessler before, a Special Agent with the Internal Revenue Service. As distinguished from a Revenue Agent who examined returns for their accuracy as purely a civil matter, special agents were assigned to cases to investigate possible criminal violations.

Hogan liked Kessler personally, but especially so professionally. Like many accountant types he had known and worked with, Kessler was a no-nonsense guy who was meticulous in his fact finding and presentations to the U.S. Attorney's office. There was no bullshit about him and you could rely on what he told you as true and based on objective evidence. Kessler neither overstated the strength of his investigation nor underrepresented what he had uncovered.

When it came to the credibility of people he encountered, Kessler leaned to the conservative side of believability. Kessler knew what juries demanded from the government in criminal cases, and the need for evidence to be compelling in meeting the standard of proof beyond a reasonable doubt.

As was his custom, Kessler appeared at Hogan's office at the precise time for the appointment. Greeting Kessler warmly, Hogan extended his hand.

"How are you Ira? It has been a while but it is always a pleasure, and invariably fruitful, to see you again."

Kessler returned the warmth and, rather than accept Hogan's proffered hand, wrapped his arms around Hogan in a bear hug and lifted him off the ground. Taken somewhat aback by Kessler's enthusiasm for the visit, Hogan asked him what he had for breakfast.

"Dan, it is not what I had for breakfast that excites me, but what it is I hope to be serving you. Not that I am not excited to see you again and work with you, but we may be sitting on a keg of dynamite that might blow the roof off a lot of places. And some of those places have been sacred up to now."

Hogan responded, "Ira, I have never seen you so affected by your work before, and I cannot wait to hear what you are about to tell me. It's not like you IRS guys to exaggerate or to view a case with such rose-colored glasses, but unless you have gone through some personality change, it must be good stuff for you to want to dance with me first thing in the morning."

"Dan, you know I am neither a blowhard nor a salesman, and everything we ever worked on before was buttoned up and unassailable. Well, I am early in my investigation, but what I have uncovered so far, and what else may be out there—well, it just seems to be too good to be true. Let me start from the beginning and see if you share my thoughts."

"Ira, it's all yours. First, let me ask if you would like some coffee."

"No thanks, I'm good."

"All right then, have a seat. I will close the door and tell my secretary to take my calls and no interruptions. And I promise not to interrupt your presentation, as hard as it is for us lawyers to keep our mouths shut."

"OK Ira, relax for a couple of minutes if you are able."

Ira responded, "Dan, you ain't seen or heard nothing yet."

On his way back to his office to hear what Kessler had to say, Hogan was struck with the swiftness with which Kessler had shattered his perception of the matter-of-fact, just the facts, ma'am kind of criminal investigator Hogan thought Kessler embodied. As he thought about it, it was more than the bear hug he was victimized by. Kessler appeared to be occupying that rare space an investigator experiences when solving a crime, seemingly without answers, or discovering a key piece of evidence that gives form to all of the other pieces present in disarray. He had never seen Kessler so buoyant, not even when he sat at the prosecution table in an earlier trial with Hogan as the jury announced a guilty verdict on all counts. It had been a difficult circumstantial evidence case, one in which the defense lawyer made a masterful final argument and acknowledged as such by Hogan and Kessler. Hogan silently told himself that no matter what Kessler would say, he would have to temper his enthusiasm so as not to prejudge this case. Hogan had seen prosecutors, on occasion, fall so in love with their own views of the strength of a particular case that would later crash against the rocks because not every stone was unturned in the investigative phase of the proceedings. Even at that, Hogan could not conceal his surprise at Kessler's attitude.

As Hogan reentered his office and sat in the chair behind his desk, he gave Kessler his best smile and told him, "Ira, it's your show."

Straightening his tie and sitting upright in his chair for his audience of one, Ira Kessler cleared his throat and began. "Dan, I have to give you a little background first, what I have found so far, and where we should go. And you can interrupt me any time you want. First, by way of background. When you and I worked together in the past, you may remember conversations we would have from time to time about various justice systems, particularly the criminal justice system. We debated which of the three branches of government was the most vital to an effective democratic form of government. I think we agreed that there was no right answer to that, but we agreed that the judicial branch was the closest to the people and had the most visible and immediate effect on the populace and those directly affected. In criminal cases, possible loss of freedom to individuals was ever present, as was, on the other hand, the safety and welfare of the community. On the civil side, a whole host of interests were involved, including the futures of children, families, fortunes and the necessities of life. Underpinning that branch of government was the necessity for honest and learned judges. You should not be able to buy your way out of imprisonment when you have committed a serious public wrong, nor should any civil case be decided by virtue of a "fix," or some other non-meritorious reason. And we both knew that in some local courts and with certain judges, results could be bought. Even stupidity could not produce some of the eyebrow raising outcomes we were sometimes exposed to."

Hogan interjected, "I'm listening, Ira, but I do not know how the IRS can audit or investigate a whole system of government with a population the size of Chicago and its environs."

Kessler answered, "Well, how about a big part of the system. You would sign off on that, wouldn't you Dan? But I'm getting ahead of the story. Hear me out."

Hogan replied, "Ira, it's still your floor. I agree with the objective you're suggesting, but tell me how to get there."

Failing to suppress a broad smile, Kessler told Hogan to "pay close attention. This is where you and your office come in."

Hogan said, "I'm listening."

Kessler resumed, "As luck would have it, one of our young Internal Revenue Agents was assigned the income tax return of Floyd Siegel.

As you must know, Siegel is a big time lawyer in this city, especially in the county and state courts. A major reason he is so famous and sought out is because his record is so tremendous. He wins regularly, and often when the odds seem stacked against him. He does mostly criminal cases, but can often be found in heater civil matters. I'm sure you heard of him.

Well, this young agent is as gung-ho as they come. He knows this taxpayer is a celebrity, so that elevates the stakes all around. But the other major factor for the agent's zeal is what the taxpayer's records look like and when he asks the taxpayer questions that need answers, he gets a blank stare or a bunch of mumbo jumbo. Siegel's major way of doing business is in cash. As often as possible, he gets paid in cash. When it comes to claimed business expenses and deductions, cash is going out the door in droves. I'm talking thousands coming in and thousands going out. And aside from bank records and certain required records kept by those he does business with, it is impossible to trace, or reconcile the income and outgoing payments. The agent does the best he can, but even he admits that he cannot vouch that his own analysis is completely accurate. But what the agent is confident of is that Siegel had to have unreported income and unexplained expenses."

Hogan interjects, "How did the examination start? Was it a routine audit?"

Kessler explained, "Nothing routine about it. The Service received a bunch of CTR's from some casino hotels in Las Vegas—you know—Currency Transaction Reports—which have to be filed with us for transactions of $10,000 or more. So that was the start of the audit. The agent asked Siegel for explanations regarding expense deductions he was claiming. He wanted back-up information as to who the payments went to and what the business reasons were for the claimed deductions. Because there was so much cash, all kinds of detail and back-up were missing. The income reported barely supports the life style Siegel enjoys. When the agent asks for back-up records and supporting evidence for expenses and compilations of amounts and sources of income, Siegel's vague explanations don't pass the smell test. As is normal procedure, the revenue agent referred the case to the Criminal Investigation Division, and it was assigned to me. I reviewed the revenue agent's report and then talked to him.

"After talking to the revenue agent and going over his calculations to make sure the tax deficiencies he had worked up were substantial, I decided to do a little homework on my own. I issued some summonses for more records from banks and other sources, and buttressed the numbers a little bit. I went to the library and got as many news clippings as they had on file for high profile cases that Siegel filed an appearance in. I read whatever content that was available regarding the nature of the case, any evidence described, the presiding judges, and the results obtained. Some of them were eye popping outcomes.

"I then made a spread sheet listing the CTR's we had in chronological order and any other detail about the trips I could find. There appeared to be, in some instances, a correlation between the end of cases Siegel was the lawyer on with the trips to Las Vegas. There wasn't anything scientific about the comparisons, but it did provide some pattern of how Siegel operated.

"After that, I invited Siegel in for an interview after telling him who I was and what my division does. He agreed to come in and did so with a highly respected criminal tax lawyer. I explained to Siegel that the tax laws favored the IRS in cases of insufficient or non-existent records; we can deny unsupported deductions. When it came to the income side, the tax code includes income from whatever source derived. His lawyer asserted that the insufficiency of records does not make a criminal case. When I replied to counsel that illegal payments made to others and income not reported on returns might well support a criminal prosecution, he declared the interview was over. He refused to discuss the question of illegal payments in any way and instructed his client to remain silent. With other claimed expenses, counsel engaged in some give-and-take with me, and argued that there were, at least, some records available to support them. When I raised the topic of illegal payments, he responded quickly—too quickly if you ask me—that there would be no discussion about that. He was noticeably decisive and firm about that. In my opinion, a little too quick and a little too firm. I think there's something there, and I would bet on it."

Intrigued by the narrative, Hogan asked Kessler what he thought was the "something there."

Kessler explained, "You know Floyd Siegel is one of the top lawyers in town, don't you? Whenever a big criminal case comes down the pike, he is almost always on it. Some of the outcomes in those cases defy reason and common sense. He deals a lot of cases with pleas and then walks away with results sometimes too good to be true. I'm not saying he is not great in front of a jury, but that is not where he works his magic. The judges seem to love him, so he takes bench trials a lot. And even when he pleads his clients, their sentences are sometimes like Christmas gifts. You and I both know that 26th and California can, at times, be tough on prosecutors. Being soft on crime is one thing, but sometimes sleeping in the same bed with big time lawyers is a little too cozy."

Hogan nodded his head in agreement, and added, "Much as I hate to think it, there are times when it seems the strength of the evidence offered by the prosecution is ignored and the concept of a second chance and rehabilitation hold sway rather than a just punishment. Even when results stink, how can you crack the relationship between judge and lawyer, even assuming there is something funny going on?"

Kessler responded directly to the hypothetical question, "One way to approach it is to threaten Siegel, not only with a fraud prosecution, but also with a long prison term if a conviction is obtained. Give him something to think about; let him compare some nights in prison with his pleasant days and nights spent in Las Vegas. Let him explain to a judge and jury why he is such a great lawyer and such a lousy record-keeper. Sometimes when you put it to guys like that with those hard choices, they fold their cards rather than run the risk of a bad loss. What do you think, Dan?"

Hogan responded, "I am definitely going to take the case for further investigation and possible prosecution. We can work it up some more so that Siegel can see there is no wiggle room on the facts and law. Siegel is no fool, and if he does not think he can beat us in court on guilt, maybe he will not want to face one of our tougher judges on sentencing. Guys who enjoy the best life has to offer may not want to contemplate the worst life has to offer. If my suspicion is right, he can tell us plenty about how he operates in the Circuit Court of Cook County. The least we can do is give him the opportunity to help himself and show him our cards and how we intend to play them. We might tell him we know he is a great lawyer, but we suspect it is not all skill he uses with some of the judges he appears before."

Kessler, visibly elated, got up from his chair and advanced toward Hogan, intent on giving him his second bear hug of the morning.

Before they parted, Hogan told Kessler that he wanted a complete report from the Special Agent along with the Revenue Agent's work-up. Along with the report, Hogan said that he wanted to meet the Revenue Agent and interview him as well. He told Kessler that the agent did a very good job and wanted to tell him so in addition to picking his brain about his contacts with Siegel.

Hogan told Kessler that as a result of the national election of November 1976, a new U.S. Attorney was going to be appointed for the Chicago office. As a result, there might be some delay in moving forward on the case for that reason. Hogan advised Kessler that he would keep him posted as events unfolded, but that he wanted Kessler to be assigned to the investigation now that it had been accepted by his office. He told Kessler nothing of importance would take place without informing him of any progress made.

Dan Hogan remained in his office with the door closed, contemplating his next move while thinking through all he had heard. The idea of probing into the county court system for evidence of criminal conduct, particularly bribery, was not new to him. Conversations through the years with Assistant State's Attorneys and their frequent complaints about some of the judges assigned there frequently occupied his thoughts. Some of their stories simply inflamed him because of results that could not be justified.

Hogan had been born on the south side of Chicago of Irish parents. He was the youngest of five children, consisting of three boys and two girls. Because his parents were strict, often viewing conduct as either right or wrong, Dan did not get away with much. As the youngest, he was the beneficiary of a lot of hand-me- downs, from clothes to books to toys. Even as the youngest, Dan never felt cheated in anything important to the family, nor did he believe he was favored because he came last. He went to Catholic elementary and high schools, with the rigor of his studies and the climate of the schools matching that of his parents. Dan knew that the rules of conduct established by his parents and supplemented by his teachers were born of love, and always felt that his personal welfare was a paramount consideration by his parents and teachers.

After high school graduation, Dan entered the seminary. Although not a rebel at the seminary, he realized he was not suited to the life of a priest and dropped out in the middle of his first year. Torn as to what his life's pursuit should be and meandering in his interests, Dan was at least certain that he should finish college and get a degree in something. So, like many others in his station in life, he chose political science as his major. He would later change to an accounting major.

There is often some event, innocuous at the time it happens, that proves prophetic when looking back in tracing the path of a life. In Dan Hogan's life, there were two.

The first of these took place in college. The curriculum for Hogan required that he take a course in speech sometime during his sophomore year of college. The course required, in addition to class participation throughout the semester, the delivery of a speech to the entire class near the end of the semester. Although Hogan was an excellent student and was not innately a shy person, the thought of standing alone before a group of his peers and delivering a speech sent shivers down his spine. The teacher required each student to select a speech given at some prior time that had gained historical distinction through the passage of time. The student had to first deliver a well-crafted speech of his or her own creation on the same topic as the historic speech by way of introduction and then recite the historic speech.

Although not an intellectual coward, Hogan could not bring himself to sign up for the class in either his sophomore or junior year of college. At the beginning of his senior year, a faculty advisor approached Hogan and told him he would be unable to graduate unless he took the required speech class. Left with no choice, Hogan signed up for the sophomore speech class.

For reasons known only to him, Hogan selected a speech once given by one of the great orators in American history, President Franklin Delano Roosevelt. At least he passed on President Abraham Lincoln.

As these things sometimes come out, Hogan's own speech, and the delivery of both, were a huge success. His teacher was so effusive in her praise that she told Hogan she could not tell when Roosevelt's speech began and his own creation ended. She even asked him if he discovered it somewhere else. Hogan assured her it was his very own. As would have been true of anyone else, Hogan never forgot her words of praise and treasured them.

The second experience that helped him chart his course in life took place during his first job after college. Although he passed the CPA examination, Hogan decided to become an Internal Revenue agent. For the first three or four years, he performed field audits of tax returns of various businesses to determine whether the correct tax was listed and paid. After that, Hogan was selected to be an instructor of income tax law to newly hired Internal Revenue agents.

It happened that the courses he was teaching were at the Dirksen Federal Building in downtown Chicago. The building housed virtually all the federal courtrooms for the Northern District of Illinois. The classes taught by Hogan required his presence in the classroom about four to five hours each day, with the rest of the eight-hour day to be spent in preparation for the daily classroom lectures. The occurrence of numerous trials being conducted daily in the same building he was working in proved to be irresistible to Hogan. He would frequently use less of his non-classroom time that was allotted and, instead, go to the courtrooms where trials were in progress. He would sit as a spectator for the remainder of his workday. Hogan was enthralled by these visits and every facet of trials witnessed. From the skill of the lawyers to the wisdom of the judges to the dignity and formality of the proceedings, he loved it all. Deciding to go to night law school was simply a decision waiting to be recognized. ⚖

After reflection on how next to proceed, Hogan settled on the next step to be taken on the Siegel case. He decided to approach First Assistant U.S. Attorney Ben Jones. Jones was an experienced AUSA who rose through the ranks based on his courtroom excellence and the view that his brilliance in court was matched by his ability to analyze issues and recommend courses of action to follow. When less experienced prosecutors needed somebody to consult with, Jones was invariably the first choice to seek out. He was the perfect first assistant and was universally respected.

Hogan paid a visit to Jones soon thereafter. "Welcome Dan. I haven't seen much of you lately. You must be busy," Jones remarked by way of welcome.

"Hi Ben, it's good to see you. You're right, I have been busy but I wanted to brief you on a particular case I was recently assigned to. The IRS presented a tax case on a lawyer named Floyd Siegel. Siegel is a very prominent lawyer, especially in the state courts. Because of the results of an IRS audit and lots of unexplained deductions, we might be sitting on a powder keg of an investigation, which I want to tell you about. I can't be sure where it will take us, but the fewer people in the know, the better positioned we will be in to keep a lid on."

"I trust your judgment on secrecy at this point, so we will limit who to share information with. So tell me what you have got, at least up to now. I do recognize the name and have exchanged a few routine pleasantries with him at various social-legal functions, but that is the extent of my contacts with him. He is by no means a friend of mine, nor is he an enemy."

"Ben, I appreciate your confidence. Let me tell you what we know, and also what we don't know. You are probably more familiar with Siegel's exploits and successes as a lawyer than I am, but I would say he is one of the best and most successful criminal defense lawyers in the city, and some of his notable successes have also come in high profile or serious money civil cases. It sometimes seems as if he can perform miracles in the state and local courts. He doesn't come over here much, but some local prosecutors think it's more than just skill at work."

Jones asked, "So what kind of case do you have, and how strong is it?"

Hogan continued, "It started as a civil audit with a real sharp revenue agent assigned to look at his return, specifically for his law practice. Siegel is a sole proprietor and he employs a full-time bookkeeper, but she does not do his returns. She relies on whatever records he gives her. She does not reconcile bank accounts, and this is especially significant since he uses cash for many of his expenses and, near as we can tell, regularly gets paid in cash. Siegel does not have very many back-up documents or other evidence to support a lot of his claimed expenses. At this point, we are not sure if his income can support his expenditures, both for his practice and his personal expenses. It needs a lot of work, but he may have omitted some of his gross income from his return. What intrigues me the most, however, is the abrupt end to his meeting with the IRS Special Agent. When the Special Agent asked him to identify the recipients of payments made in cash in connection with his law practice, both he and his then lawyer representative refused to talk about that topic in any way and declared the interview to be over when the question was put. This was after the Special Agent made a point of saying illegal payments were not deductible.

"I know you should not read too much in body language and to rely on suspicion rather than cold, hard, irrefutable evidence, but refusing to answer a relevant question rather than try to explain it or offering to try to reconstruct the records tells me a lot. That reaction tells me Siegel has something to hide, and the lawyer knows what it is. It was the lawyer who declared the interview over and directed Siegel to not respond to any other questions."

"So, what do you propose to do?" asked Jones.

"What I would like to do is call him in for an interview with his lawyer. I will outline the strength of our evidence and our intention to buttress or expand it with as many records and as much information as we can assemble. As it stands now, the tax deficiencies are quite substantial. We will tell them when that process is complete. We intend to indict and convict him and ask for the longest possible sentence we can reasonably justify. I will tell him that we believe he has made illegal payments to perhaps judges or other officials, in an effort to help his clients. I will tell them that if that is so, and if he is a party to judicial corruption in any way and is willing to be entirely truthful about that topic, the possibility of a deal will be put on the table. One way or another, I would like to know where he stands and what he can give us generally. No deal will be offered or promised at my meeting, and any proffer of information, whether general or specific, will be forgotten and not usable by us if a deal is not struck. In other words, we will not buy a pig in a poke or deal in the blind. For him whatever he may tell us is for bargaining purposes only at this point and nothing more. Tell me what you think."

Jones responded, "At this point, I think that your approach is a good way to proceed. Quite frankly, it is the only way to proceed. The outcome of the election will affect our office and what we can do in the future. We will have a new U.S. Attorney in Chicago and a new Attorney General in Washington, D.C. Whatever informal approval we might receive early on will be subject to later reviews of what we have already done and what we plan to do. We are going to have to see what each of these officials have to say about our project, methods contemplated, and plea agreements to be offered. All of that necessarily assumes, of course, that we develop evidence to support federal prosecutions of local lawyers, judges, and whoever. So I think you can proceed with him as you outlined, with the clear understanding that if Siegel has something we want and need, we will discuss his own case with him and we will need to enter into a formal agreement with him in order to finalize terms. Your proposed meeting with him should be viewed as informational only and subject to a final agreement between him and us."

With a smile on his face and a heart beating with gratitude for the okay from Jones, Hogan walked out of Jones' office as only a newly advised prospective father could—happy as a lark. ⚖

Shortly after his conversation with First Assistant U.S. Attorney
Ben Jones and his approval to call in Floyd Siegel and his lawyer for a
meeting, Dan Hogan called Ira Kessler. In any circumstance in which an
AUSA meets with a prospective subject or target of an investigation,
it is always necessary for the AUSA to have at least one other person at
the meeting on the same side as the AUSA. The best choice is usually
the investigative agent who presented the case to the U.S. Attorney's
office. That agent is not only the most knowledgeable person about
the facts developed to date, his presence at an interview serves a number
of functions. The agent can supply background material to help
develop questions to ask in the first instance and follow-up questions
as the need develops. The agent is also in the position to challenge
or contradict statements made during the interview by the subject as
necessary. Additionally, the agent can be used as a later "prover" of what
was said at the interview. This is important in cases of conflicting versions
of interview statements, because the AUSA conducting the interview
and the presumed prosecutor after any indictments are returned
cannot be a witness in any case in which he is acting as a lawyer.

For all of these reasons, Ira Kessler was called to ensure his
availability at a meeting to be arranged with Floyd Siegel. Hogan got
Kessler on the phone and began the conversation. "Hello, Ira, how are
you? It's Dan Hogan."

Kessler responded, "It is good to hear from you Dan. How are you
doing? Have you made any progress on our boy?"

Hogan told him of his conversation with Ben Jones, and his approval
to go ahead with a meeting with Siegel if he was willing to come in.
Hogan said the purpose of the meeting was to see if Siegel was willing to
discuss ground rules for a later in-depth interview session, along with a
general assessment of what Siegel had to offer in any investigation of
others. Hogan told Kessler how important his presence at the meeting
would be, particularly as to Siegel's apparent credibility, and knowledge
about other criminal matters, and its potential value to the government.

Kessler said, "Dan, I am willing to make a friendly wager with you—maybe a nice steak dinner with all the trimmings–that he will play the game with us and it will be a great result—and more than we can imagine. If you are happy with what he gives us, you will buy me dinner. If not, it's on me. Do we have a deal?"

Hogan responded, and tried to act restrained while contemplating the future. "Ira, if he turns out half as good as I hope, you can pick the restaurant. We will make the call to him and set up the time and place for the meeting. My stomach is starting to rumble already. I sure hope you win the bet, Ira. I'll let you know the details. Stay hungry."

Trying to suppress his excitement and reverting to his professional demeanor, Hogan called Floyd Siegel to arrange, what he hoped it to be, the first of many meetings with a man with a rich and hoped for informative past. Siegel agreed to Hogan's invitation to meet, and told Hogan he would have his lawyer with him. Hogan told Siegel that IRS Special Agent Ira Kessler would also be in attendance. The time and date were set for Dan Hogan's office.

Less than a week after Hogan received permission from Ben Jones to proceed with Floyd Siegel as discussed, Siegel and his lawyer were escorted to a meeting room in the U.S. Attorney's office. In addition to Dan Hogan, Special Agent Kessler was present on behalf of the government. As Siegel entered the room, the rich cut of his suit and his bearing upon entrance, even more than his acknowledged reputation, spoke volumes about his success as a lawyer. Not far behind, in both appearance and reputation for success, was Arlen Neal. Neal's practice was centered at the federal level in criminal cases, particularly in white collar and tax cases. He was known to be a tireless preparer and often the lead counsel at multi-defendant trials with an enviable success rate. Although federal criminal defendants in Chicago were usually convicted, whether by pleas of guilty or by jury verdict, Neal's record of success was better than most other defense lawyers. In public presentations, he was known to be both methodical and eloquent. In his private dealings with prosecutors and other defense counsel, Neal was known to be a man of his word and if given, would be reliable in his honor of it. He was a tough competitor, but relied on his skill for success rather than bluster and bravado.

Hogan introduced himself to Floyd Siegel and Kessler to Neal, and greeted Neal with appropriate respect and manner. "Thank you both for coming in what I hope will be beneficial for all of us," said Hogan upon everyone being seated. "I have arranged for some coffee and rolls, and if anyone would like something else, just tell me."

Neal then thanked Hogan for his hospitality and added the following. "We hope you are right when you say this meeting might be beneficial for all of us. Naturally, it is only my client's benefit that I am interested in, but I realize that unless you are helped in some way, you will not have much, if anything, to offer us. How do you propose we proceed with this meeting?"

"We have discussed it among ourselves and I propose the following terms," replied Hogan. "I think you will agree that this is fair to both sides. We will ask questions of your client. Anything he says will only be used for evaluation of what he knows and is willing to offer us by way of information. We have no recording devices of any kind and will only consider what he says for purposes of a deal to be considered and discussed at a later time, including with people in the chain of command or those working with them. If the Government and you and your client are deemed to have important information to us, then we will meet again and discuss the terms of an agreement binding on both sides. Only if such agreement is reached will we be free to use the information your client gives us for our purposes. If no agreement is reached between us, then this meeting today will be as if it never took place. We agree that anything your client tells us will not be used for any purpose whether against him or anybody he names about whom he has knowledge. We think that this is the fairest way for us to proceed. We need to have an idea of what your client can provide, since the importance, depth, and breadth of what he can tell us will help us in assessing both his value and the terms we might agree to. I think you will both agree that this is the fairest and best way for both of us to go forward. By virtue of your reputation Mr. Neal, we believe you to be a straight shooter. We intend to act in the same way, and I think you will agree that is reflected in our proposal. May I also add that we expect honesty and candor from your client, not necessarily as a future Government witness, but as someone who is knowledgeable and truthful about unlawful events so as to permit further investigation without experiencing "detours, I don't remembers, or maybes." I know you understand that, but I want to make sure he understands that.

"Let me also say security is utmost in this relationship. For example, even within our office, I have given you a pseudonym," looking directly at Neal's client. "You will be Rex Reed for our purposes, and anything you tell us will be shared only on a need-to-know basis. And I would, obviously, suggest the same for you. You would have no value to us if you start telling others—anyone at all—of this or any other meetings with us. Besides that, and you know this better than I can describe it, your own security and that of your family would be severely jeopardized should you go public regarding your role with us. So those are terms I offer, the same for both of us and fair to both."

Neal answered, "I appreciate your presentation Dan, and I do agree that it is fair and workable." Addressing his client, Neal said, "Well, I guess you just got baptized with a new name, Rex. What do you say about the terms proposed for today?"

"Like you, Arlen, I think they are fair. I just have one question. Will I have to review movies?"

Grinning broadly, Hogan replied, "When I picked the name, I wanted it to be simple and different. I did not even think of that other guy, to tell you the truth. But no, no movie reviews."

Siegel, stifling his own chuckle, said, "That clinches it. I am willing to go ahead, even though I have lots of opinions about the movies and the movie business, but agree that that name and occupation has already been appropriated. So let's get on with it."

Hogan then got down to cases. "First off, I want to tell you how strongly we believe in the strength of our case as to Mr. Siegel. We do not offer our perspective to browbeat or bludgeon you in order to secure your agreement to assist us. We do not believe that would reflect the respect you are both entitled to in these discussions or to the process we are engaged in at this time. We believe that would be counter-productive. But you are entitled to the honesty of our beliefs and to our future intentions should no agreement be reached between us.

"The IRS agents have worked very hard in building a case against you. Revenue Agent Lagger and Special Agent Kessler believe the tax case is unassailable. The evidence shows some unreported income which we can prove through the bank deposit and cash disbursements method, and the figures do not lie. Of even greater significance to the bottom line of tax due and owing, however, is the lack of evidence in support of numerous deductions claimed for supposed business expenses. Not only is there a lack of documents in support of the claimed deductions, there is no basis to determine the recipients of the payments, the nature of the payments made, the purpose of the payments, or their legality. You both know that the claimed deductions must be reasonable and necessary under the tax code. Those two terms, "reasonable and necessary," have been defined to exclude payments illegal in nature. Bribery payments of any kind, and irrespective of to whom made, are clearly not deductible, and that holding has been the law for as long as anyone can remember. So those kinds of payments and claimed deductions cannot be said to have been mistakenly claimed or negligently so. I know you both know those things to be true, along with our view that juries in criminal tax cases would have no trouble following that principle of law when they have to deliberate a verdict. Quite frankly, and for reasons we do not need to express, we believe those are the very kinds of payments being claimed on the tax returns of Mr. Siegel. Should no agreement be reached between us, it is our intention to prosecute Mr. Siegel for filing false income tax returns for at least three years, perhaps more, and underpaying his taxes by a substantial amount of money."

Arlen Neal responded, "My client and I are fully aware of all you just expressed, and your unstated position that if a conviction results, your request for a stiff sentence will be the expected consequence."

Addressing Siegel, he asked whether he was willing to answer the Government's questions under the stated ground rules with any final agreement as to use of the information subject to later discussion and resolution. Siegel nodded his head in acquiescence.

For the next two hours the newly named Rex Reed offered his bill of particulars about judicial corruption in the Circuit Court of Cook County, Illinois. The reactions to what they heard by Hogan and Kessler were similar. As servants of the law and the virtue it represented to both of them, it was a disheartening cornucopia of misconduct by a variety of public officials of every rank in the system. As criminal investigators and prosecutors, Reed's knowledge of it and the promise of usable detail was a treasure trove of prospects for good.

Although yet unnamed, "Operation Greylord" was given birth. ⚖

The national election in November 1976 resulted in a new president being elected, and who would take office in January, 1977. Because the new president was from a different political party than the incumbent, the ripple effect of having a new leader in the executive branch of government was deep and far reaching. Of significance to the law enforcement community in the Northern District of Illinois, and particularly the City of Chicago and County of Cook, was the appointment of a new United States Attorney.

That was not surprising, since tradition and protocol dictated that all United States Attorneys in the entire country were to submit their resignations to the President, who would then be free to retain any incumbents or to appoint new ones. The choices made were invariably done after consultation with the relevant senators and members of the House of Representatives from the state and region covered by the district office with geographic jurisdiction.

The selection of the new U.S. Attorney in early 1977 was a surprise to most people of the district. Instead of choosing a person with a prosecution background or similar government experience, the President selected Brandon Hartnett to be the new U.S. Attorney, the chief law enforcement official in the Northern District of Illinois. The surprise came from the fact that Hartnett had been one of the leading criminal defense lawyers in Chicago with a record of success almost without equal.

Hartnett was an unexpected choice. Some views held by uninformed citizens was that a lifetime criminal defense lawyer would not be tough on crime. Those thoughts did not take into account the universal view of Hartnett among those who knew him well and others who opposed him in court, that Hartnett was a man of integrity in all his dealings with clients, prosecutors, and other defense lawyers. His success as a lawyer was the result of his extraordinary skill in the courtroom with a work ethic to match. Many people simply failed to appreciate Hartnett's belief in the devotion to his client's cause, whether it be to an individual criminal defendant, citizen plaintiff, or merely a cause undertaken for the welfare of society. Vigorous advocacy was never confused with professional integrity necessary to the performance of his duties, whether to an individual or institution of government.

It was Assistant U.S. Attorney Hogan who, after doing some preliminary work on the case presented by IRS Special Agent Ira Kessler, and meeting with Reed and Neal, requested a meeting with U.S. Attorney Brandon Hartnett. Invited to the meeting with Hogan was First Assistant U.S. Attorney Ben Jones, who had been wisely retained by Hartnett. Hartnett opened the meeting, "Good morning, Gentlemen. It's bright and early, as you requested Dan. The fact or nature of this meeting has not been disclosed to anyone, also as you requested. For present purposes and until I decide to the contrary, this subject shall be confined only to personnel who have a need to know information, and what they can be told is limited to what they may themselves be directly involved in. We all know about leaks in this town, and lots of them start with something inadvertently mentioned. So, let's hear about what we've got."

Ben Jones then responded, "Brandon, I think it's best for Dan to start since he is the one who debriefed someone I will refer to as Rex Reed. Reed said he wanted to make a proffer of information to us in order to help himself in his own investigation. Dan has talked to him for about two hours, so we thought we better bring it to you at this point. We are just at the early proffer stage, and we have not made a commitment to Reed, but he's getting anxious. I think we know enough about what he has to offer, and it is probably a good time to make a decision for us, and also for him. I don't want to get too excited this early, but this could be something really big for us."

Hartnett, addressing Hogan, then said "Dan, take it away."

Hogan took the floor. "Let me first describe who Reed is and how we got to him. He is the subject of an IRS criminal investigation which started when one of the major casinos in Las Vegas filed some CTR's— Currency Transaction Reports—over the course of one week for this guy a few years back. As you know, those reports are required when a person engages in a financial transaction with a casino for $10,000 or more. I don't know if Reed knew about those reports and just didn't care, but in any event, the IRS jumped on the case. At first, it was just a civil examination with no thought of criminality. But the agent who was working the case was top notch, so after he digs awhile he realizes that the CTR's are just the tip of the iceberg. The agent uncovers all kinds of cash transactions going every which way, a lot coming in from his clients and a lot going out to who knows where. The income is, of course, taxable, but the expenses and expenditures are iffy. We don't know where they're going or for what purpose, let alone how much it adds up to. The guy's books and records are a disaster, but that hurts Reed a lot because we can reconstruct his income based on how much we can prove what he spent and the assets he has accumulated. What he cannot do, however, is claim business expense deductions unless he can prove the amount expended and that it was for a legitimate business expense. To be tax deductible, expenses have to be reasonable and necessary under the law. It has long been held that any payments made that were illegal in nature are not deductible. When the agent starts pressing him for the identities of the recipients, the amounts paid, and the purpose of the payments, Reed starts to clam up. So that agent starts calculating the gross income for each year under audit—now expanded from one year to three—and each year's income is a big number. And then the agent tells Reed that unless he identifies the recipients of his claimed business expenses and can prove it was a legal and legitimate business expense, he cannot deduct the expenditures on his tax return. So imagine how he must have felt—a whopping income every year for three years and practically no deductions available to offset the income."

Hogan began to walk around the room while continuing his narrative, full of excitement and nervous energy. "Reed tells the agent that he is going to put Reed in bankruptcy or the poor house. Of course, the agent tells him he put himself there because he can't, or won't, come up with the required evidence to support the deductions. It was at this point the agent decides that, because of the numbers involved and Reed's refusal, or inability, to tell him who he is paying and why, the agent decides he may be sitting on a criminal tax case. In that circumstance, the agent is required to refer the case to the Criminal Division of the IRS, which will then assign a Special Agent to take over the case from the Revenue Agent. When that happens, it becomes a criminal investigation, although the Revenue Agent stays on the case to assist the Special Agent. When the Special Agent contacted Reed and asked him to come in for an interview, Reed came in with a prominent criminal defense lawyer. He basically said he was a poor record keeper, but the expenses were real. When Reed was asked to identify some recipients of cash payments, he refused to do so and ended the interview. Reed's case was referred to our office for criminal prosecution. Reed then hired Arlen Neal to represent him before our office.

"Besides the numbers, here's the other thing I could not get out of my mind. This guy is a big-time lawyer in the state—perhaps the biggest. Although he handles mostly criminal cases, even civil litigants run to him when the stakes are high. Naturally, he is so busy because he is so good, at least from a results analysis. Sometimes too good, if you get my drift.

"The other thing to consider when it comes to his success, things that travel through the grapevine, is some serious grumbling by state court prosecutors about how he does it. A few insist that he just can't be that good in some cases where he gets great results. These few complaints about him do not come with proof, so it could just be sour grapes by poor losers.

"But the thought is out there that it's not all skill at play. That sometimes he plays by his own set of rules. You understand that this was all speculation on my part, but what fosters the thought is that Reed is the proverbial hale fellow well met. Popular not only among his fellow barristers, but with lots of judges as well.

"Reed is regularly seen at judges' campaign events and, based on reports they have to file for campaign contributions received, Reed drops a lot to many of them. He is also seen frequently at favorite restaurants and bars where the criminal lawyers hang out, including sitting judges. These are places where a reputation as a big spender is made."

Hogan continued. "As you well know, Neal is as good as criminal lawyers come in Chicago. I reached out to him and asked if he would consider making a proffer from Reed. Neal offered to bring him in on the following conditions: Reed would answer all of our questions truthfully; he would not hold anything back. If we were satisfied with his truthfulness and the scope and nature of his information, he would not be criminally prosecuted for anything he told us about tax violations or other crimes. Neal realized Reed would have to pay taxes on what he owed IRS as a civil matter, along with penalties and interest, and committed Reed to doing that. Neal said that if they could not reach any agreement with us along the lines he proposed, then the proffer information could never be used, directly or indirectly, against Reed or anybody else Reed mentioned in the proffer statements. In other words, Neal's position is that if there is no deal, it will be as if there never existed any proffer sessions. Neal, of course, understands we are free to discuss what he told me with you and anybody else in the chain of command necessary to making a decision on his deal request but, once a decision was made, his true name will never be revealed to anyone. In order to be on the safe side, I chose to rename him Rex Reed so that nobody accidentally slips up and uses his name. Reed and Neal say that concerns about the safety of Reed and his family are real because of what and who he knows and has dealt with."

Hartnett then responded, "Dan, I think you have handled it well so far and I compliment you. Giving up criminal prosecution altogether of Mr. Reed is a big price to pay for what appears to be a major tax cheat, so the question is what do we get in return?"

"Brandon and Ben, I know that you have been in the criminal law business in this city for a long time and have certain suspicions and questions about whether the local court system operates the way it is supposed to. We see conviction rates in some criminal courts nowhere near what they should be, we hear grumbling from prosecutors through the grapevine bitching about some judges and some decisions, and we see constant efforts in Springfield to give prosecutors the right to a jury trial in criminal cases just as defendants have that right. There have even been some attempts in isolated cases to find out if certain judges are being bribed, only to have those prosecutors brought before the Attorney Registration and Disciplinary Committee and get slapped down for their attempts. As we all know, when a transaction takes place between two crooks, it is hard to crack the relationship and get one of the two to open up with the truth. I don't want to mislead you about Rex Reed. He is a sleazy and crooked lawyer, a tax cheat, and an apparent briber of judges. Besides that, he is a cheating husband and father, lives life in the fast lane, uses drugs and booze to excess, and chases women when they don't chase him. He would make a horrible witness in court. But if you were looking for someone who knew the most about sleazy judges, bailiffs, court clerks, police officers, prosecutors, and other criminal defense lawyers, based on first-hand knowledge, Rex Reed would be your guy. Because of his long tenure of practice in the state courts, his prominence among defense lawyers and his stable of clients, he is the one who can detail not only his own corruption, but that of many, many others. Reed's tales would, if properly investigated and corroborated, blow the lid off the perceived sanctity of the criminal justice system in the state courts of Cook County. Because Reed has so much personal and professional baggage as a witness, I don't think we can use him to testify at trials in cases we indict. Another reason against using him is once he is exposed as a government source in the investigation of corruption in the court system, evidence would disappear, leads would dry up, and our ability to control events would disappear. Making cases using only historical evidence may be good in a small set of cases, but the attendant publicity would operate to preclude gaining evidence across the full scope of criminality which we have good reason to believe exists. While I believe Reed would be a lousy witness in court and a punching bag for good lawyers in light of all he has done, in my opinion he has been truthful so far in describing to us what he knows. Using Reed's information as leads in our investigation will save us a lot of time and manpower. Besides, juries might have a tough time believing him. There's also no doubt in my mind that this is a "must go" investigation, that nothing we can do is as important as cleansing the criminal justice system from these creeps and restoring some needed faith to the conduct of judges and lawyers. Reed has named at least ten judges that have accepted bribes to fix a variety of cases in state court. He suggests even more judges than that, especially in traffic court and in the handling of drug cases. Of the 10 or so judges named, Reed says he has directly given money to at least 5 of them and, as to the others, has given the cash to their bagmen. Besides the judges, he has named upwards of 20 court personnel—docket clerks, bailiffs, police officers, and others— he has given cash directly to them to pass on to their judges, as well as some cash for themselves. Besides the court personnel, he has given us the names of a number of criminal defense practitioners who are crooked—in excess of a dozen—and the names of some prosecutors who have accepted bribes."

"He has so much experience in the courtroom he also knows who is honest and who is not. This information is also important to us besides knowing who can be trusted; we can direct our investigative efforts away from them. Although we have not had much time or opportunity to do so, we have been able to verify by other evidence, including circumstantial evidence, some of what he has told us. Although he has no reason to lie to us at this point, he has been told that if he does lie to us, the deal would be off for that reason alone. Both he and his information appear to me to be credible and believable. Reed also admits that based on his conversations with other defense counsel, there are other corrupt court officials he has not dealt with, even as extensive as his own experience has been in the system. If we make the deal and use him as proposed, his name should never surface, nor will we have to publicly defend using him in the court of public opinion since he will never testify in any trial we bring. As you can clearly tell, I am quite enthusiastic about taking on a broad-based investigation of judicial and related corruption in the state court justice system with the use of Rex Reed's information as a starting point. What we have to gain exceeds by the widest margin imaginable what we would be giving up. For me, it is not a close call. I'll defer for now the way we can use Reed and the structure of any investigation we undertake."

Hartnett then said, "Thank you, Dan. That was an excellent presentation of the work you have done and the results achieved so far. There's lots of promise there. What do you think, Ben?"

Jones then answered, "I share Brandon's view that you have done quite well so far, Dan. I commend you. I don't need to be a flag waver in the presence of two men who share my passion for helping right the wrongs of society we encounter or devoting my time and energy to trying to make life a little better and fairer for all of the citizens we serve."

Jones paused and searched for words. "I know the three of us in this room share the same conviction and desire. That is why we are here together in this room, and on the same side. In all the years I have been a trial lawyer, I have always assumed, and wanted to believe deeply, that the judges I was appearing before were all fair, honest, and devoted to resolving cases based solely on the evidence before them. Whatever my suspicions may have been from time to time, I acted in accordance with my beliefs. There is nothing in life I hold more dear than the honesty and integrity of the civil and criminal justice systems in this country. That is why it is so disheartening to hear Dan's report of Reed's interview. And that is why the decision before us is so easy for me. As stated by Dan, we have so much to gain in our pursuit of the corrupt, and so little to lose by a single less prosecution who, at the least, will have a civil price to pay for his sins."

Hartnett then responded, "I think it is a little unfortunate we did not tape our little meeting this morning. The eloquence with which you both expressed yourselves is worthy of memorialization. I agree this is a must-go investigation, and the terms of Rex Reed's cooperation are acceptable to me. That is the easy decision. The harder decision is how we proceed."

Jones, having the most prosecution experience of the three men in the room, then said, "Even as Dan was describing the value of Reed, at least the initial value, it is the leads he provides as to what to look for, where to look, and potential defendants that are important. I think if we start subpoening witnesses to appear before the grand jury and documents to be produced there, all in an effort to uncover historical facts about old cases, we will not be successful. Word will get out about the nature of our investigation as soon as we hand a subpoena to the first witness. Witnesses will decline to testify as is their privilege under the Constitution, documents will disappear as past experience reflects, and others will immediately suffer from a permanent case of amnesia. The investigation will be short and not so sweet, at least for us."

Hartnett then asked, "What do you see as our alternatives?"

Jones answered, "Active cases in the system, control of cases in their development, and resolution. There are two ways to do it with active cases. One way is to use real cases in the system involving real defendants who may have committed real crimes. These cases would be the vehicles to see if judges could be and were fixed, with the development of evidence as it was generated and recorded. The necessity

for us to control things would be available to us. So what is the downside to using real cases? There are many. The first and obvious one is that a real defendant who had his case fixed may get wise or suspicious as to what was done in his case to bring about his acquittal. But more than that is this possibility: a real defendant may be a real criminal in general. Bringing about his freedom to allow him to commit a crime at a later date, perhaps a quite serious one, could never be justified. The risk to us of that happening, and the possible harm to an innocent victim that may ensue, could never be overcome by the reward of the prosecution of a court officer. That calculus is obvious. The alternative to using real cases to uncover crimes is the creation of phony cases to place into the system to be manned by undercover lawyers where possible and undercover law enforcement officers playing the part of parties in these made-up cases. The desire to control events is enhanced, although it still creates risks for both the undercover lawyers and agents. Undercover lawyers would necessarily have to lie to judges and others in court proceedings generated by fictitious events and parties; the risk of losing a law license by lying to a judge, albeit in a contrived case, is quite real. The ethics rules governing lawyers do not contain an exception for investigating a judge suspected of corruption."
Jones looked around the room to gauge the reaction to his suggestions. He then continued, "The risk to undercover law enforcement agents acting as party participants in phony cases may sometimes result in the jailing of the undercover agents and being ensconced in the midst of real criminal defendants in jail for real crimes. As you can see, none of our investigative methods or choices are fail-safe. The question is which of these methods provide the greatest possible successful outcome versus the least amount of risk. One of the virtues of using active, albeit phony cases, is the ability of undercover agents and lawyers wearing wires when conversing with subjects under investigation. As you know, recorded conversations of criminal targets are the strongest proof available at a trial. They can be done solely with the consent of

one party to the conversation—the agent. The other investigative tool afforded by real-time cases is the ability to wiretap phone conversations between suspects and others or place a bug in or near locations where suspicious conversations are taking place, even without one party consenting to the recording device. Using Rex Reed's information in this way can be done even as his anonymity is preserved in keeping with the terms of his deal. I know we don't have to decide methods to use in this meeting, but the alternatives do give us plenty of food for thought. Those are my present thoughts."

Hartnett then reacted. "I think Ben has covered our choices should we go forward, but suggest we give the topic further consideration. Gentlemen, it has been a long and productive meeting. I want to thank you for your invaluable contributions. My decision to proceed in the investigation is firm. My leaning as to method is the use of fabricated cases. That requires further thought on everybody's part, as well as the input of the FBI Special Agent in charge of the Chicago office. They will have to do a lot of the heavy lifting, not to mention the assumption of enormous risks. We will have to apprise them of the situation and secure their cooperation. Something tells me they will find the prospects as exciting as we do. Till the next time. Thank you again."

The meeting was adjourned. ⚖

Harry Meredith was a long tenured Special Agent of the Federal Bureau of Investigation. Born and raised in rural Indiana, his formative years reflected two great passions. Although his talent in sports was modest, he exhibited a fierceness of desire and effort when involved in sports that made up for his lack of talent. Nobody wanted to play him in any one on one sport because Meredith would never quit no matter the score.

Meredith's other passion involved schoolwork. He was fanatical when it came to being the best student in class. The only difference with schoolwork is that Meredith was a gifted student as distinguished from having only mediocre skill in sports. His zeal for excellence in the classroom was the same as on the playing field. The only difference was the skill level.

Meredith served in a number of FBI field offices. In each of those positions, his reputation for investigative skills and tenacity produced a series of promotions to leadership positions. When merely a field agent, he was assigned to participate in the ill-fated investigation known as Abscam. Although widely viewed as a failed exercise within the confines of the FBI, Meredith had no role in the concept, planning, or execution of the investigation. His only duties were involvement in a few interviews and, when Abscam ended, his burgeoning reputation as an investigator remained intact.

Meredith had been appointed Special Agent in Charge of the Chicago office in the mid-1970s. A characteristic of his leadership skills was the close working relationship he had with the United States Attorney's Office and other state and local law enforcement agencies. Particularly respected were his communication channels and information sharing with the Cook County Sheriff's office and the Chicago Police Department. The historic mistrust between the feds and the locals in the law enforcement realm, while not completely eliminated, was no longer a barrier to the efficient use of resources. Although Abscam was an undercover operation, Meredith was also significantly involved in the murder investigation of three civil rights workers in

Mississippi during the turbulent 1960s. Even though the FBI may have been unpopular with local officials during that investigation, Meredith's professionalism and fearlessness in pursuing the perpetrators earned both him and the Bureau the respect they deserved for carrying out their mission.

A few months after being appointed the United States Attorney for the Northern District of Illinois, Brandon Hartnett requested that Meredith attend a meeting in Hartnett's office. No mention was made of the purpose of the meeting. Also invited to the meeting were FBI Assistant Special Agent in Charge Martin Mitchell, First Assistant U.S. Attorney Ben Jones, and AUSA Dan Hogan.

As the FBI contingent entered Hartnett's office, he greeted Meredith and Mitchell warmly. "Nice to see you both. I think you know Ben Jones. I want you to also meet AUSA Dan Hogan, who I do not think you know." Meredith and Mitchell greeted the three prosecutors with equal warmth.

Hartnett addressed the gathering. "I wanted to meet with you both without any fanfare and without publicizing it to any other personnel, either from your shop or mine, what the purpose of this meeting is. Ben and Dan are already privy to the information I am about to share with you but, as you will soon see, secrecy is paramount here. If you sign on to the project, you will understand why."

Meredith responded, "Brandon, although we do not know each other well, I know enough about you that trust is the key ingredient to you in relationships among partners. You come highly recommended to your position. And if we haven't already said so, we have the same desire regarding those we work with."

Hartnett replied, "The feeling is quite mutual. So I am just going to get right into it."

"Thank you," offered Meredith.

Brandon commenced. "We have a case under criminal investigation in which a very prominent and successful lawyer who practices mostly in the Cook County Circuit Courts, especially in criminal courts, is facing some serious criminal tax problems. We think we have a terrific case against him and we were getting ready to indict him. He went and hired a top-notch criminal defense lawyer, well respected, successful and a straight shooter. The lawyer has reached out to our office, and we agreed to hear his client off the record and hear his proffer about what he knows and can tell us about judicial corruption in the local courts. In a nutshell, he can tell us plenty. He has paid bribes directly to a number of judges for favorable rulings and paid a number of bag-men for other judges for the same reason. He can tell us who the bad guys are and who the good guys are. He is such a corrupt lawyer, though, that his word—especially if it's the only one—is not good enough to indict and convict who he has fingered. We need to gather other evidence in some way to make strong cases against these crooks. We can't use him as a witness because of his tremendous baggage and because of whatever deal we have to cut with him, but he's invaluable in his knowledge of extensive corruption and his ability to direct our attention as to who to go after.

"On the assumption that we would use historical information to make cases on past, completed events, the first subpoena we would issue would bring a halt to the investigation because of the publicity it would engender. Evidence would dry up or disappear and the witnesses would all probably contract amnesia. Then we considered using real cases now in the system with real criminal defendants as witnesses, but that would be an enormous risk of later harm to society. Besides, we could not overcome the publicity problem."

Meredith interjected, "I agree with both of those concerns."

Hartnett continued, "So if we want to push the investigation, we could create phony cases, get them before the targeted judges, and see what happens. We would need you and your people for that effort, and we would have to assume lots of risks too numerous and serious to contemplate at this time. There you have it."

Meredith then spoke. "As you may know, I had an operational role in Abscam which, by all accounts, was a bust. It was also a black eye for the Bureau. It seems you are suggesting a somewhat similar type of undercover operation. Of course, in Abscam, we were flying blind. Here, you've got a guy who can personally describe bribe payments, so we have a good basis—probable cause, if you will—on who to go after. That's a huge difference. Of course, creating phony cases is doable, but if you want to get in front of suspect judges, are you talking about phony arrests but possible real incarceration for the undercover agents?"

Hartnett replied, "That would surely be a risk. We could minimize it in various ways which we can discuss later, but we certainly could not eliminate the risk entirely."

Meredith responded, "I understand. But if I see the picture right, we've got a whole lot of lying going on—to judges, and while under oath. Some by undercover lawyer agents, pretend parties and pretend defendants. Who is going to insure no prosecution of our people for perjury, making false statements to judges, or preservation of real law licenses?"

Hartnett then said, "Harry, you have identified some of the key problems in this approach for your agents and our lawyers. I agree with your concerns. And to make things even worse, the necessity of secrecy reduces, if not completely eliminating, our ability to truthfully explain things to whoever we need to if something blows up and somebody is in real peril of physical injury."

Meredith then said, "Well, I certainly appreciate your candor and your refusal to sugarcoat the downsides. On the other hand, there is no reward without risk, and it sure is depressing to think all of that corruption is at the level you've touched on. Who knows how far the corruption goes, but it sounds awfully bad. And one thing I already feel strongly about just listening to you speak—if things are as bad as that lawyer says, and he almost certainly does not know all of it—we just cannot let it go on. We have to find a way to stop it. That is what we are in business for."

Hartnett responded, "Harry, I sure do appreciate your careful consideration of this summary, and I am especially heartened by your reaction to what appears to be taking place in the local courts and the judicial system. No matter what your decision is, I want to thank you in advance."

Meredith said, "I will honor the secrecy pledge, but you know that I have to let headquarters know of your request and, of course, get the Director's approval for a go. By the way, do you have a name for the operation?"

Hartnett replied, "As a matter of fact, I came up with one just the other night. I have had trouble sleeping lately, just thinking about this case; what it's about and where it may lead. I thought about our judicial system, where it came from, and how it compared to mother England. As you know, over there judges and barristers wear horsehair wigs and elaborate and decorative robes. The rhetoric used in court can be formalistic and arcane, and pomposity sometimes intrudes on their dignity and scholarship. The term "Greylord" seems to fit snugly in describing their proceedings. In contrast, this investigation is a peek into our judicial conduct and proceedings at their basest level, where evidence matters not at all in the outcome of cases, where corruption is king and results are determined by money, where the concept of justice for all is replaced by the demand of cash for one. To me, the contrast is stark and the irony irresistible. So I thought we should call it "Operation Greylord." What do you think of that name, Harry?"

Meredith replied, with a look of amusement beginning to frame his face. "I think that it's a great idea. Nobody will connect that name and all it connotes to a federal investigation of sleaze engaged in by some of our most important public officials. I'm on board with it."

In a matter of days, Hartnett received a telephone call from Meredith. Meredith said, "Brandon, I want you to know that the Director has approved our involvement in Operation Greylord. My top people here

are also anxious to participate and, indeed, quite enthusiastic.
As we both recognized at our meeting, the details of our involvement
need to be thoroughly considered and prepared to the nth degree.
There will be a multitude of adverse possibilities in the events
contemplated, so much work remains in order to minimize risk.
Non-Chicago resident agents will certainly be required, and we have
the o.k. to procure temporary transfers. There is more to be discussed,
but I will await your office's leadership on what to do and when.
I am personally excited about our involvement. I want to again thank
you for your approval and so looking forward to working with you.
We are going to make everyone forget Abscam. Till later." ⚖

Peter Theos was the son of Greek immigrant parents. Both his father and mother emigrated to the United States after World War II and the equally ruinous civil war which took place after the conclusion of the world war. Peter's parents became naturalized citizens of the United States in due course, while Peter's birth in this country conferred his citizenship automatically.

Although the hardships of the German invasion of Greece were not spoken about often by his parents, when they were talked about with other relatives, they left indelible impressions upon Peter. Nothing inspired emotions and passions among his parents and relatives than when they were describing the horrors visited upon the Greek people by the conquering German army.

Able-bodied men were often rounded up and herded into village squares upon the merest suspicion of resistance to their oppressors, there to be machine gunned to death in the presence of their wives and children. Suspicions asserted by the captors were often pretexts for the elimination of men generally, with decisions of who should die the product of whim and nothing more.

Daily life featured the care, comfort, and feeding of the occupying forces. The consequent deprivation to the citizens of the country, especially in the towns and villages, was irrelevant to the German commanders. Concepts of law, order, justice, and fair treatment for the local population were neither part of the lexicon of the occupation forces nor reflected in their conduct.

Listening to these stories, accompanied by the tears of the elders, often left Peter questioning the veracity of what he had heard. As a young man growing up in America, it was difficult for Peter to credit the depth of devastation the descriptions offered up, even if by people he loved. And then to hear that after the Nazis were finished killing the Greeks, the Greeks started killing each other in the civil war. It was sometimes just too much to bear.

The Theos' still had many relatives in Greece and both Peter and his parents wanted him to go there and meet them. Peter was anxious to go. Money was saved for the trip, letters were written about the upcoming visit, and itineraries planned. Although Peter would travel to Greece alone, a host of meetings with relatives and friends in diverse cities and villages awaited him.

When Peter returned to America three weeks after he left, he was a changed person. Whatever doubts he had about the stories he had heard about the hardships and devastation suffered by Greeks disappeared from his mind. The tales told by aunts, uncles, and friends of Peter's parents who lived through the war years were even more vivid, and more horrible, than he heard in America before he left.

Peter knew he would never forget his experiences from his visits nor would he fail to remember the tears with which the stories were told. In each town and village he visited, erected in the central square of each was a concrete monument listing the names of each villager executed in cold blood. The atrocities of the Nazis were memorialized forever in Peter's mind.

The ravages of both wars took its toll on the country. In spite of the ultimate victory by the Allied Forces in the world war, the destruction visited upon the country made the prospects for its future bleak. Virtually all families suffered loss of life to one or more members, and the idea of emigrating to the United States by Peter's parents had taken deep root. The civil war cinched the decision.

Peter's parents came to America laden with hope for the future but not much else. They knew very little English, had few skills, no guarantees of employment, little wealth, and few relatives. The same could be said, of course, of most Europeans flooding the shores of America around the same time.

Peter's father and mother understood the necessity for and value of education in their newly adopted country. Although their schooling in Greece was meager, they understood instinctively how important it was to Peter's success in America. The ways of village life in Greece were ill-suited to the dynamism America was in the midst of at all levels of society. Besides, the school system in America was the best in the world, and much of it was free.

Peter's attendance at college was a foregone conclusion; there was never a thought he would not go. There had never been discussion at home about post-college education or career paths, however. Peter's teen-age trip to Greece left a variety of indelible impressions, and nobody had to tell him how important education was to his future.

Peter knew before the trip that he owed his parents much. For them to leave the land of their birth, to bid goodbye, probably forever, to learn a new language, to forget old and treasured customs and learn new ones, were sacrifices made by them for him as well as for themselves. He could never alleviate the hardships they confronted. All he could do, and would do, was to honor their lives with his devotion to the welfare of all people in America, immigrants and natives alike.

Peter's trip to Greece brought home to him, in ways vibrant and real, the ruination of a country with a lawless society. The rule of law was non-existent during the war, and only the force of arms commanded the lives of all, both the victors and the vanquished.

Peter decided to dedicate his life to the law, to help bring it where it was lacking, and to prosecute it when justice demanded. The absence of laws based on reason, fairness, and equality was, for Peter, the prescription for the kinds of destruction wars and other conflicts inevitably produced.

Peter would devote himself to the common good rather than pursuing and amassing wealth for himself. Not only would he honor his parents in this way, he would honor the country of his parents' choice. When he returned from the trip to Greece, he knew the time to decide his calling in life had arrived and his future was ordained. Peter would go to law school and pursue a career in public service. Upon graduating from law school, he applied to be an Assistant State's Attorney. He quickly established his credentials as an excellent prosecutor.

Peter Theos was the Assistant State's Attorney assigned to prosecute the defendant Moe Sands for the possession with intent to distribute two kilos of cocaine seized from Sands' car. He was in the courtroom when Judge Lunden announced his ruling granting Sands' motion to suppress the evidence.

Judge Lunden, in adding insult to injury, condemned the credibility of the two police officers who found the drugs. The judge said Sands' testimony was more likely to be true. No mention was made of Sands' prior drug convictions or his motive to lie. Theos flashed back to his parents' stories about life in the old country and the absence of law worthy of respect.

A few days later, and while still stewing over Judge Lunden's ruling suppressing the drug evidence in the case against Moe Sands, Theos received a call from Assistant U.S. Attorney Dan Hogan. Although Theos and Hogan had never met, Theos had heard good things about Hogan, but was mystified as to why Hogan was calling him. A meeting was arranged for Theos to meet with Hogan at his office, with Hogan requesting Theos to say nothing to anybody, including his superiors, about the upcoming meeting. Theos agreed. ⚖

"**Good afternoon, Dan.** It's nice to meet you," said Theos.

"It's also good to meet you, Peter. I've heard good things about you. Having said that—and meaning it—I know you understand that even though we are doing similar kinds of work, I can't tell you the specifics of what I'm involved in. Since you have the same obligation to your superiors and to your office, I am sure you understand. It has nothing to do with whether I trust you.

"I know you are curious about why I reached out to you. So I will share with you some general information that I know you will hold in confidence. We have received some information, not yet verified and not usable in a court of law, that the judge you now prosecute cases in front of, Judge John Lunden, may have acted corruptly in the past. We are quietly pursuing that information to see where it takes us. If we reach an understanding for your cooperation with our investigation in that area, I will fill you in on what we know and how we know it. We are not at that point yet."

Theos responded, "I am perfectly aware of both of our obligations of secrecy. I assure you I do not seek any confidential information you may have, nor do I intend to disclose any on my part. I will say I find what you just said both interesting and exciting. I have my suspicions about that judge, especially because of a recent motion to suppress hearing and how the judge ruled. I would be glad to share with you what is going on in my court. To be blunt, I was sickened by his ruling, but there is no place I can go to but here."

"Have you tried talking to your boss, the State's Attorney, about what you see and think? As far as I know, he enjoys an excellent reputation for honesty and integrity, and would seem to be trustworthy."

Theos responded, "You are right about him—he is a good man. But it is just not possible, or practical, for him and our office, to investigate defense lawyers who oppose us in court and judges who preside over our cases. It would be practically impossible to keep any such investigation a secret, and the first public disclosure would bring a firestorm of criticism. It would be political suicide for an elected state's attorney to allege improprieties by lawyers who are on the other side of our cases or judges who may rule against us. That we are engaging in sour grapes when we lose would be the mildest of epithets directed our way. For us to do so, we would never make it to first base in the gathering of evidence, and "sore loser" would be the new middle name of my boss."

Hogan replied, "I sure can't argue against your assessment. There is something to be said for our federal system with the U.S. Attorney holding office by appointment by the President of the United States and his appointed AUSA's owing allegiance only to the office they hold. We don't have to please any political party or its members. Our clients are the citizens we serve and the independent bosses who guide our efforts."

Theos said, "I believe deeply in what you say, and that is the way law enforcement should behave. But we just can't start investigating people we deal with on an everyday basis, our adversaries and those whose decisions decree our successes and failures."

Hogan added, "I want you to assume my office and I are most interested in what you have to say and that we promise you our confidentiality in your visits to our office and our conversations. I see no conflict in listening to what you have to say and none on your part in telling us about those things you believe to be illegal and corrupt. We will do nothing to compromise you or your office and will keep you apprised of what we plan to do with anything you tell us. If those terms are acceptable to you, I want to confirm them with the U.S. Attorney and to schedule a meeting at your convenience."

Theos stood and said, "Let me also say I have every confidence that an enormous amount of good will come from this and, in the end, we will all be the better for it. It's going to be a long road, but one worthy of the destination." ⚖

Encouraged by Peter Theos' enthusiasm and manner at the meeting, Hogan arranged to have U.S. Attorney Hartnett meet Theos and speak directly to him about the investigation planned. Because secrecy was so important, the meeting was to be held in a motel room in a near western suburb of Chicago. Only three people knew of the meeting: Hartnett, Hogan, and Theos.

"Good morning, Peter, it's nice to meet you," said Hartnett, extending his hand.

"Good morning Peter, it's good to see you again," said Hogan.

"Good morning to you both. As you may have guessed, I have been doing a lot of thinking about our last discussion. In truth, I am consumed about its prospects and can barely think of anything else."

Addressing Peter, Hartnett said, "Peter, I know what a momentous decision this is for you, and if everything comes out as we wish, it will be life changing for us all. We know how bright you are, Peter, but our proposition requires much more than smarts. We know you have considered all the possible consequences for you, but we just want to make sure you fully understand what it will take on your part and how it will affect you both while you are working for us, but also when it is all over. We want you to go undercover for us. But it's not just secretly working on our behalf, it's also being willing to change your reputation from squeaky clean to one willing to act dirty when you have to. We are investigating crooked judges and lawyers. We want you to get close to them, befriend them, act interested in doing what they do in order to make money. Being undercover will not help us unless the bad guys start to think you are one of them instead of being Mr. law and order. Do you see that?"

Peter responded, "I fully realize how I will have to act. I have thought endlessly about my ability to do that, in addition to the risks that will confront me."

Hartnett tried to paint the future, "It is almost a certainty that you will never be able to practice law again in the Circuit Court of Cook County, whether our project is a success or whether it is a failure.

Recording people and lying to them will all be made public at the end, and many will never ever trust your word or honesty again, not even some of your friends. That will be true, even as it is established that you were always on the side of the angels. The fact that you pretended to be a certain person but were really someone else will always follow you; it will have an indelible quality to it. You may also lose your law license."

"I cannot imagine you have ever done anything like this before," added Hogan.

"No, I sure haven't." "Have you ever acted before in school or anywhere else?" asked Hartnett.

"No, never."

"A major test of your success will be how convincing you will be in going from a clean as a whistle guy to somebody who would sell his honor for a few bucks. Your reputation as an honest prosecutor is going to make it that much harder for you to convince certain people that you are as bad as they are; that, somehow, overnight, you concluded that the law was something to be dishonored, not honored," explained Hartnett.

"I fully appreciate that, but I'm sure I can do it."

Hogan added, "You have such a great reputation now; do you think you can handle it when even some of your close friends start believing you are a kink and want nothing to do with you. I know you fully understand how nobody—I mean nobody—can be told of your true role. Maybe your girlfriend can be told, but that's it."

"As long as I have her, I can deal with it."

Hartnett continued, "You know you will have to make friends with lots of people you might not choose as friends, and some of them you will have to get awfully close to. You are probably going to come to like them—some perhaps quite well—eat with them, drink with them, go to their weddings or the baptism of their children. Maybe even sleep in their homes. You're going to have to get them to trust you implicitly in order to share their corruption. And then, if all goes well for us, you will have to betray them. Do you think you can handle that? Do you have the stomach for it?"

"I realize that thinking about doing something and doing something are two different things, but I believe I can. I also know I can become fond of a person even as they engage in corrupt conduct that so offends me personally and professionally. What it will be for me, as well as for all of us, is that we value honesty and integrity above all other considerations even, perhaps, the deep friendship and affection of another. I know you can like a dishonest person, find him charming and engaging and want nothing bad to happen to him. But if I am to believe in the sanctity of the law and the pursuit of justice as a noble calling, then I cannot pick and choose when to hold those things sacred and when they must yield. If I close my eyes to misconduct for reasons of friendship, it is not much different than if I close my eyes for reasons of money."

Responding, Hartnett said, "Peter, I am not trying to discourage you from joining us. God knows I believe you have the strength and wisdom to help us and we want you to do that and be part of the team. We just want to be fair with you and point out the downsides to your role. We have not even raised the risks to your own safety should your role be disclosed. This is serious conduct on the part of those we may target, with possible consequences as bad as can be imagined. Loss of income, loss of license, family disruptions, even loss of freedom. The more successful we are, the worse the consequences to those we catch. In these circumstances, personal safety is an issue and while we will do all we can to keep you safe, there are no guarantees."

"Brandon, I am fully aware of the possibilities should things go south—I willingly assume them as far as my own safety goes. As for the rest of it, I assure you I can handle it and am up to the challenges. As I have faith in you and in the project, I ask you to have faith in me and my abilities. Count me in."

"We're glad to have you," responded Hartnett.

Extending his hand, Hogan said, "I very much look forward to working with you. I know it's going to work out for us." ⚖

Peter Theos was debriefed by Dan Hogan upon acceptance of Theos' commitment to join the federal investigation. A main topic of discussion was the recent drug case Theos prosecuted in Judge Lunden's courtroom involving defendant Moe Sands. After describing the case in detail to Hogan, Theos expressed his strong suspicion that Judge Lunden was fixed in the case.

The discussions ultimately centered on the wisdom of putting Sands' attorney in the Grand Jury and giving him immunity, thereby compelling him to testify. If he testified truthfully, his statements could not be used against him in a criminal prosecution. If he refused to testify, he would be held in contempt and jailed until he agreed to testify. The third alternative would be a denial that he engaged in bribery. If and when evidence later developed that he did bribe the judge, Spencer could be prosecuted for perjury before the Grand Jury.

The tactic under consideration was one used in Chicago by the Strike Force unit of the United States Department of Justice in the 1960s. Its investigation centered on syndicate crime activities and, among other things, resulted in Sam Giancana being subpoenaed before a federal grand jury. Giancana was believed to be a top leader of the mob, and by virtue of the subpoena and the concomitant bestowal of immunity, was given the Hobson's choice of answering the prosecutors' questions under oath or refusing to do so and being held in contempt of court by virtue of the refusal.

Not surprisingly, Giancana declined to testify, resulting in a contempt citation and imprisonment for about one year. He was released as a consequence of the expiration of the grand jury's term of existence. Apparently believing a new grand jury was going to be empaneled with a new subpoena to issue for Giancana's appearance, Giancana decided to leave the country and travel to Mexico and other Latin American countries in apparent fear of a replay from the Government. He remained there until he was seized by police in Mexico and shipped back to the United States in 1974. About one year later, he was murdered in his own home while with apparent friends. The crime was never solved.

In order for the Government to get evidence against Judge Lunden, it would have to give up the ability to prosecute Spencer if he did in fact bribe Judge Lunden. Because it was far more important for the Government to go after a corrupt judge than a corrupt lawyer, Hogan agreed with Theos that Spencer should get immunity. U.S. Attorney Hartnett, when advised of the Hogan-Theos recommendation, agreed to do so.

As a result, a meeting was arranged with Saul Spencer, who was advised that he could bring a lawyer with him, and that it would be a good idea to do so.

Present at the meeting for the Government was U.S. Attorney Brandon Hartnett and Assistant U.S. Attorney Dan Hogan. Along with Saul Spencer was his attorney, Henry Armstrong. Both men were asked to keep the meeting invitation confidential for reasons to be explained at the meeting.

Hartnett opened the meeting. "Good morning, Saul and Henry. I appreciate your acceptance of my invitation to come and meet with us."

Hogan added, "Good morning. I know it is unusual to meet with you in this way, but Brandon will soon explain why we invited you to come to see us like this."

Armstrong returned the greetings. "Well, good morning to you both. I will admit to more than a normal share of curiosity as to why you wanted to see Saul in this way, but I am sure you will answer that in short order."

Spencer added his own greetings, and his curiosity. "Good morning, gentlemen. I too admit to a high level of curiosity about the purpose of this meeting, and the intrigue regarding your request to keep it a secret until our discussion. Let me say, in candor, it was a little disconcerting to get this hush hush request to meet like this without some explanation of the need for both secrecy and immediacy."

Hartnett answered, "I understand completely, and I will get to the point right away. But first, we need to have an agreement, for your welfare and ours, that this meeting is entirely off the record. There are no recording devices on our end, and I want your assurance that there are none on your end either."

Armstrong responded, "I give you my word that neither I nor my client are equipped in any way to record this meeting. Is that right, Saul?"

Spencer answered, "You both have my word on that matter—no recordings on either side."

With those assurances, Hartnett continued, "The next thing I would like from you both, and to be reciprocated by us, is to keep this meeting and what is discussed private among ourselves; no public discussions about what is said here and the nature of anything we tell you. I want you both to understand that we will promise not to use anything you say here in any way to prosecute you or to present at any public trial or public forum. Anything Saul says will enjoy complete immunity by our office and any other law enforcement agency which somehow becomes informed of it. While we do not expect that to happen, I will offer you an insurance policy against any use of the information—should we receive any from you—that would be harmful to Saul in any way."

Armstrong responded, "Brandon, I know you are an honorable prosecutor and your word is reliable, but how can you guarantee the conduct of others?"

"We will put it in writing and tell you in advance of any intended use we would like to make of it."

Armstrong replied, "It sounds like a fair enough ground rule on which to proceed, and I so advise my client. But what you want to know from Saul, what you are investigating, and what you think he can give you, are still a mystery to both of us. If you need our commitment before we proceed further, I can understand that in order to simply have a conversation. Of course, it is Saul's decision to make. For my part,

I am ready to agree just to learn more about what you are trying to get at, but I think we can put our toes in the water. What do you think, Saul?"

Spencer answered, "Like Henry, I trust your word, but need to get it in writing to protect myself. I still don't know what the hell you're after, and whether I can, or should, help you, but I am baffled by this mystery you have created with all this secret stuff that I sure would like to know about."

Hartnett explained, "That is understandable, but we need your acceptance of our terms—which I assure you will benefit you in a great way if you agree. We promise not to use anything you tell us to prosecute you, and you will learn that that promise will prove very valuable to you. But we need your commitment to secrecy and full cooperation and truthfulness in what you know to make it happen. If you want to talk to Henry privately before you decide, we will make a private office available. But unless we have the deal in hand that I put on the table, I will bid you both a pleasant morning and we'll each go about our business. If you like, you can give us a tentative agreement so that we can make you aware of what we are about, and so long as you promise to maintain the confidentiality of that, we'll give you some information that will be helpful on what you decide to do."

Spencer said, "I can ask Henry for his advice as to your last offer of a tentative agreement now; I don't need a private office for that. Do we, Henry?"

Armstrong addressed Spencer and Hartnett, "No, not at all. Since we do not know the subject you are talking about or Saul's role in it, it is necessary for us to know that to give you a definitive answer to your proposal. My advice to Saul is to tentatively agree to your terms so we can evaluate all the pros and cons involved in the circumstances. This should not be like a poker game where nobody knows the cards in everybody's hands before you bet the future and go all in. Your proposal, near as I can guess, will have some major consequences to Saul and his family. More relevant information from your side is absolutely necessary for us to play our hand. But even that tentative decision lies with Saul, and I don't see that we're giving anything up by listening to what this is all about."

Spencer then agreed, "Since I'm sitting here on the edge of the chair provided by the Government, I will agree to the terms of the proposal for now so that I can quit guessing what's up with you."

Hartnett noted their acceptance of the terms of secrecy, "That's fine. Before you leave here today, you will have our written commitment about secrecy and non-use in hand. I know you and Dan have met as adversaries in the courtroom and that you have a sense of each other. You should also know I have put Dan in charge of a highly sensitive investigation regarding subject matter and the profile of the potential targets. Dan is better equipped to tell you about our investigation and where you fit in."

Hogan then said, "Saul, I am going to be both direct and blunt with you so that you and Henry can make a realistic assessment as to your exposure here. We believe you have fixed some cases you have handled in state court by paying cash bribes to certain judges for the outcome you wanted. The most recent case we have knowledge of involves a judge named John Lunden and your client Moe Sands."

Spencer reacted emotionally, "That's outrageous. I am not a fixer. The Moe Sands case was, fortunately for Moe and me, before a judge who is a strong proponent of the Constitutional rights of citizens and opposed to overreaching in search and seizure cases by the police."

Hogan responded, "Saul, save your bullshit and spare me the theatrics. The Constitution had no more to do with Lunden's ruling than your imminent appointment to the Supreme Court of the United States. Lunden claimed to believe a two-time convicted felon—a major drug dealer—over two of the finest police officers ever to wear the Chicago Police Department uniform. These two guys are not only terrific cops—10 honorable mentions for services while police officers for both—besides each getting an Army medal for valor in combat action while serving overseas. We've had Constitutional scholars look at the facts of that case, and to a person they agreed the search and seizure in that case was lawful. Even the judge had to agree with the conduct of the officers; it was by the book. The only way the judge could pitch the case was to call the officers liars and not rely on the methods they employed. And you know what else—there was not one thing in their respective testimonies or the circumstances of the search he could point out and hang his hat on. So he didn't. He just called these two honorable cops liars and did not offer a single objective reason to justify his contemptible holding. Good thing Judge Lunden was sitting down and draped over by a robe so nobody could see his reaction while delivering the present you bought and paid for. Sometimes it's hard to fashion a straight face and conceal a quivering soul when you are doing the devil's work. And that is what Judge Lunden was doing."

Spencer reacted, "So you want me to be the pawn in your move against the judge, is that it?"

Hogan answered, "That's only part of it, Saul. You have been defending criminal cases in state courts for a long time. I doubt there are very many judges you have not appeared before. You know—and I strongly believe—that Judge Lunden is not the only judge you have fixed through the years. I only have strong suspicions whether that happened; you know if in fact it did. So the deal we're proposing is your full cooperation and truthfulness about the extent of corruption you know about in the judicial system, from clerks, courtroom deputies, police officers, other crooked lawyers and all the judges."

Spencer asked, "And what's in it for me?"

Hogan answered, "You get a complete pass for all the criminal conduct you tell us about: no prosecution, no jail, and no fines."

"What about my law license?"

"Not within my power to save for you. Also not my wish to see you keep it. Your conduct at the bar of justice up to now has not earned you a reenlistment."

Spencer asked, "And what if I do not take your deal?"

U.S. Attorney Hartnett answered. "Our plans are to build a stronger case against you for the drug case you handled before Judge Lunden. We know you have appeared before him on another drug case and won it. That result smelled almost as bad as the Sands case. We intend to put Moe in the grand jury, perhaps immunize him, and see what he says. We're not crazy about using a major drug dealer as a witness, but choices have to be made as to who is most important to go after. Right now it is Judge Lunden—and other judges. Next in line come the crooked lawyers."

"Is that all?"

"No, I'm afraid not."

"What else is there?"

Hartnett explained, "We know the drug business practices and that drug dealers deal almost exclusively in cash. They pay their bills in cash, and some of those are lawyers' bills. Cash is easy to hide, and the IRS has signed on to devote full resources to our project. If you are an honest income tax filer, you will have nothing to worry about. If you are not an honest filer, you'll have plenty to worry about. I promise you that."

"You mean you would single me out to investigate?"

"Exactly."

"You know as well as I do, you cannot engage in selective prosecution."

Hartnett responded, "It is not selective prosecution to investigate those lawyers who we have reason to believe are crooked and prosecute them. We will select every one of them we can make a case on. That kind of selection is what my office is commissioned to do. And good luck finding case law or other authority that says we cannot do that."

"So you're going to play hardball with me?"

Hartnett addressed the question, "Listen to me, Saul. The minute you quit using your legal skills to win cases and decided to trade those skills in for cash bribes to whoever would take them, you forfeited your right to complain about hardball, as you put it. No decent citizen would agree with you, and no federal jury would side with you. Those are the rules in the game you chose to play, and we will let honest judges and juries of your peers call the balls and strikes in the corrupt game you personally selected."

Armstrong interjected, "So that I am perfectly clear as to what you are offering, Brandon, please restate it."

"These are the terms we are proposing: From Saul Spencer:"

Hartnett picked up a paper from his desk and read.

"1. A full and honest recitation, as detailed as possible, of all the judicially related corruption he has personal knowledge of and personal participation in.

2. A full description of all the judicially related corruption he is aware of and the source of that information, including particulars.

3. An accounting of all cash received from criminal defendant clients for the past five years as well as cash disbursements of the funds received.

4. Full cooperation in meeting with federal agents and being debriefed on all of the designated subjects.

5. Truthful testimony at any trial in which Spencer has relevant knowledge and information to the issues presented at the said trial.

6. Full payment of any income taxes due as a civil obligation after any civil audit for returns filed or due for the last five years."

Hartnett continued reading from his notes. From the Government:

"1. Full immunity from any federal or state criminal prosecution based, directly or indirectly, on any information given to the Government by Saul Spencer, whether by interview, testimony, documents, or in any other form.

2. That no independent criminal investigation of Saul Spencer will be undertaken other than verification of information supplied by Saul Spencer, or in corroboration thereof. Other terms:

3. The immunity bestowed by the Government and the Court shall not apply to any lies or falsehoods given by Saul Spencer to the Government. Lying to the Government or its agents shall render this

agreement between the Government and Spencer null and void.

4. The intentional withholding of relevant information from Spencer to the Government shall also render this agreement null and void.

5. The Government assumes no obligation to assist Saul Spencer in the maintenance of his license to practice law or to influence the proceedings before other agencies in Spencer's maintenance of same."

Armstrong appeared shaken. "That's quite a comprehensive list of terms you just rattled off. You look like you've done your homework." Hartnett responded, "I cannot emphasize enough for you both how important this investigation is to us and for the community we serve. It is our top priority. Maybe you think we've been too tough in our demands and, as you put it, playing hardball. What I want you to consider, especially you Saul, is how destructive your conduct has been to the cause of justice. When these cases are publicized, the whole system of civil and criminal justice will be tainted. Honest judges will be indistinguishable from corrupt ones, and our system of government, regarding the intimate relationship between the government and the governed, will be viewed with disdain. At its core, democracy will be the loser and the moral high ground necessary to our ordered civilization will disappear. The stain will not be easily removed or overcome, and we will have cheated the generations to follow of a legacy worthy of admiration."

The meeting ended on that note. ⚖

A follow-up meeting was scheduled for two days hence. This meeting was also attended by Hartnett, Hogan, Spencer, and Armstrong.

Hartnett greeted all: "Good morning, gentlemen. Would anybody like coffee?"

Hogan said, "Good morning, Henry and Saul."

Armstrong returned the greetings. "Good morning to you also. I'll pass on the coffee."

Spencer, clearly unhappy, said, "I sure hope this turns out to be a good morning, but I feel you have put me between a rock and a hard place. I'll pass on the coffee."

Hartnett responded, "Saul, you may see it that way, but I didn't put you there. The first time you decided winning was the most important thing to you and how you won and got your guy off did not matter—or apparently trouble you—you put yourself there. I am not going to pretend this is going to be easy for you, but when you put your client's cash in the judge's pocket, you gave up the right to complain about your choice if you should ever get caught. I'll save my sympathy for those kids who buy Moe's dope and begin the ruination of their lives."

Armstrong asked, "May I ask whether you have talked to Moe Sands?"

Hartnett replied, "You can ask. We haven't talked to him yet, but we plan to, whether Saul takes our deal or not. If we have a deal with Saul and you, we want to use Moe to corroborate what we believe Saul will tell us. If we don't have a deal, we will move against him and make his choices much harder. I want to remind you both again that these discussions are confidential, okay?"

"Both Saul and I understand that. It is certainly not in our interest to blab. You mean you would try to prosecute him? How can you do that? Judge Lunden suppressed the evidence."

Hartnett answered, "We still have lots of options with Moe. They can still appeal the judge's ruling, although winning would be a long shot. We both know credibility determinations are the province of the judge. There are some rare cases when the Court of Appeals throws out the judge's finding. They're not planning to appeal because it would take too long and the odds are not in their favor, but it is a thought. We also do not want to create public speculation that we think Lunden is a bad judge, and that is another factor."

Armstrong asked, "So what does that leave you with?"

Hartnett responded, "We have a couple of options. One is to threaten him with an IRS investigation and prosecution. We know he is a big drug dealer and deals with lots of cash. We know what he owns—at least what is in his name—and the cars he drives. His reported income cannot remotely support what he owns and what he must spend. The cash expenditures theory of prosecution is alive and well, and we may take Moe to school on that theory. Another choice is to simply throw him in the grand jury and give him immunity. Moe will not know what we have on him, and we will make it quite plain to him that if he lies to us, his immunity goes out the window and he could be criminally prosecuted for lying. The way we see it, Moe is a big drug dealer, but we don't think he's a big gambler. We don't think he would lie to us and take a chance on what we know about him or what we can develop. Moe's got a lot of guys working for him and none of them are taking home anywhere near what Moe is making. If Moe is out of the picture, there will be a hell of a scramble to take his place. You can bet a lot of guys would like to see him go, especially his two top guys. None of these guys have ever taken an oath of loyalty to him or anybody else. In that business, it's every man for himself."

Hogan then added, "It's ironic that our system of crime and punishment—especially incarceration—is premised on deterrence. If you put the top guy in jail, those below him, in theory, would be deterred. The reality is that often, the guys just below the top guy wouldn't mind seeing him disappear for awhile so that they can move up the chain of command. Just like legit business, where the CEO has lots of people just waiting to succeed him. The CEO's departure produces two feelings for those below him: sorry to see him go because he or she was well liked, but also happy to see him go because of the vacancy created."Hartnett responded on a lighter note, "My boy Dan here is starting to get cynical with us. Go ahead, Henry, and ask him what he knows about business and the corporate world."

"I don't need to do that, but I take it that you would plan to use Moe in any event to not only corroborate Saul should he testify at trial, but also possibly as a hammer at Saul if he takes the deal and gives you bad information."

Hogan replied, "That's probably right. Much as we would hate to use a big drug dealer for any reason, on balance, his corroboration of Saul's story, should he choose to tell it, in addition to putting pressure on Saul to be truthful with us, militate in favor of getting him to be a witness, baggage and all."

Spencer plaintively said, "You must understand how difficult this is for me. My life as a lawyer is over. I will be shunned by friends and some family, and the prospects of physical harm to me and my family is very real."

Hartnett spoke to Spencer's anguish, "I cannot sugarcoat it, Saul. You have assessed it correctly. You will be giving up a drug-dealing client, or more, a crooked judge, or more, and who knows how many other crooked court officials, including some police officers. Based on your decision and the risk assessments from all quarters, we might have to discuss a witness protection program and possible relocation of you and your family. I promise that we will work with you on that. As you can see, secrecy is necessary at this point and will serve us all."

Spencer then asked, "Isn't there some way I can salvage my law license? How am I going to support my wife and two little kids?"

"We cannot offer you that. You will have to see if our immunity can stretch all the way to a civil regulatory proceeding in a research of the law or if there is some other way to salvage your license. If you cooperate with us, we will make that fact known to the licensing authorities and how helpful it may prove to be, but that is the most we can do.

The rest is up to you and your lawyer. The more you give us, the more valuable your assistance should prove to be. So what is your decision? Time is not your ally."

Spencer surrendered. "I do not see I have much choice; I will accept your terms."

Hartnett then addressed Armstrong, "Henry, I'll ask you to confirm that you have rendered fully all of the advice you were asked to give, and that your client fully understood the terms of our offer and its possible consequences."

"Saul fully understood the terms of the offer. As to the possible consequences, we discussed what we could surmise about them. As to what they may turn out to be, time will tell. I will say Saul understands all of the risks and is willing to assume them. The alternative to your offer is, as the British might put it, most unsatisfying."

Hartnett stated, "I want to set up our first interview session as soon as possible, but I need to know two answers. Did you bribe Judge Lunden in the drug case, and how much did he get?"

Spencer conceded, "I did, and Judge Lunden got twenty-five thousand."

Hartnett then ended the meeting, "Thank you both." ⚖

As a follow-up to the Spencer agreement, a meeting was scheduled to discuss the wisdom or necessity of pursuing Moe Sands as a witness against Judge Lunden. In addition to Hartnett and Hogan, First Assistant Ben Jones, Executive Assistant Sheri Vusic, and Peter Theos were also in attendance.

Hartnett opened the meeting, "In case you have not all heard, we have made a deal with Saul Spencer in the Greylord case. Spencer gets immunity for his cooperation and testimony, and he gets a pass from any criminal matters he tells us he was involved in. He has to tell us everything he knows about judicial corruption and understands the absolute need for secrecy and confidentiality; he knows that serves him as well. I want to stress again that all of you in this room are the only ones who know what we are doing in Greylord. No other AUSAs and no non-participating FBI agents know. I know it's tough to keep information away from your fellow prosecutors, but it is an absolute must in this circumstance. I will fire anyone from my shop who can't keep their mouth shut. The full scope of our work will never be accomplished if word gets out about what we're doing. We have confirmed through Spencer that he fixed Moe Sands' drug case with Judge Lunden with a cash bribe before the judge suppressed the evidence. Spencer told us that his initial fee from Sands was $150,000."

Vusic, surprised, said, "Wow, that is big-time money."

Theos explained, "It was big-time money because of the big time sentence Sands was staring in the face."

Hartnett picked up the discussion, "But that's not all. After Spencer got his 150 Gs and sized up the case better, and coincidentally had a chat with the judge, Spencer went back to Sands and hit him up for another $50,000. Out of the 50, Spencer put $25,000 in cash in an envelope he gave to Judge Lunden. So there you have it—the market price of justice in a two kilo drug case—$50,000. Ironically enough, the wholesale price of two kilos of cocaine in Chicago is pretty close to the 50. Besides bringing you up to date on the Spencer business, I wanted to get your views on whether we should use Moe Sands to corroborate Spencer at a trial of Judge Lunden. What are the pros and cons of doing so? Peter, you are the closest to this question. Why don't you go first."

Theos responded, "The obvious pro argument is that we have another witness in the bribe chain who can testify as to the source of the money and it's intended purpose—to buy an acquittal."

Vusic then asked, "Can Sands testify that Spencer told him that the money was going directly to Lunden and not somewhere else?"

Theos said, "No, he can't do that. Spencer was careful when talking to Sands; Spencer implied that some extra money was needed for an acquittal, but told us that he told Sands he could not guarantee it. In fact, Spencer said he promised that he would return the $50,000 to Sands if there was no acquittal. Spencer wound up getting paid a total of $200,000 from Sands, of which $25,000 went to the judge."

Vusic then questioned, "If Sands cannot directly implicate Lunden in the fix, does he add that much value or strength to our case? We would wind up supporting a drug dealing witness who got off scot-free on a big drug charge by buying his way out of trouble. On top of that, the only way we can get him to testify for us is to give the creep immunity from prosecution for both of the crimes he committed. Talk about making a deal with the devil. He skates out of trouble in return for testimony the jury may or may not believe."

Theos added, "Let me also paint the picture even worse than Sheri describes it. Spencer told me that when Sands testified at the hearing on the motion to suppress, Sands admitted he lied on a key fact about the traffic stop. Sands testified that the dog was called in to sniff after the drugs were found and not before. The officers had testified that the dog came to the car before they conducted the search, and that is when the dog alerted to the drugs. It was only at that time that they did a complete search of the car and found the hidden drugs. The dog alerting to the drugs was part of the probable cause needed to legally search the car. Sands told the judge the dog came after the seizure, giving Lunden a basis to disbelieve the officers, credit Sands' version as the truth, and find the search to be illegal. Sands was smart enough to give the judge something to hang his hat on, which is exactly what Lunden did. So now Lunden can say, with a straight face, that he believed the drug defendant Sands and, impliedly, suggest the officers lied. As we now know, Lunden's straight face when ruling for Sands made him $25,000 richer."

Vusic replied, "If I have this straight, Sands probably committed three crimes:

1. He possessed two kilos of cocaine with intent to distribute;

2. He aided and abetted the bribery of a state court judge presiding over his criminal case; and

3. He committed perjury while testifying before that judge which enabled the judge to suppress lawfully seized drugs from his car. Did I analyze that correctly?"

Theos said, "Right on, Sheri. And if you throw in his two prior felony convictions, Moe Sands should be, by rights, a five-time convicted felon. How's my math?"

Hartnett, in a serious vein, said, "The math is right, but the issue before us has some other considerations. As bad as Sands is, we only put him on as a witness because of what, ultimately, Lunden did. Lunden freed him, an immoral creature who preys on addicts, kids, and other sad cases simply to make money. We don't sponsor his activity on the streets. It is guys like Spencer and Lunden who give him license to take advantage of people who need help to get off drugs, not to provide them to buy. If this is to be a morality play, what side are we on? The State's Attorney tried to put the bastard in jail, and it was Lunden who kept him out. And Lunden did not act out of any noble Constitutional principle like letting a guilty man go free in order to insure a truly innocent man does not get punished. No, Lunden's version of a noble principle is to put a big fat wad of money into a bulging pocket so that a creep like Sands can keep selling his poison to the unfortunates who are in our midst."

Jones then said, "That sounds like a good final argument to me. Although Sands and Spencer will be our witnesses, in a line-up of good versus evil people, they line up right next to Lunden and not next to us. We may have had the obligation to call them, but only because Lunden, in the first instance, chose to cast his lot with them, not with us. We tried to put Sands in jail, but Lunden kept him out. Even though we did not know about Spencer and his corruption, when we did find out, we had to make a decision. Should we try and prosecute him, a private lawyer, on the word of a drug dealer, or should we use him to prosecute a sitting state court judge? Who as between Spencer and Lunden should be stopped? Who should be eliminated from doing harm to society: a public figure who hears hundreds of cases a week and has the potential to wreak havoc on an untold number of lives, or a private lawyer who will certainly be put out of business and his days of bribing judges coming to an end, just by publicly testifying and admitting the scope of his own private corruption? Even using Spencer as a witness has a societal benefit, and putting Lunden out of his sordid business, by whatever measure is used, has the greater value."

Hartnett summed up the discussion, "I agree with all of those sentiments supporting the use of Sands as a witness. As despicable as he may be, it is important to our purposes as to what he says. He clearly corroborates Spencer's version of events, one crook supporting another. Distasteful, yes. Believable, also yes. I say we make the attempt to use Sands and give him immunity if necessary. We almost certainly would have to offer it. The other choices are to not use him at all and avoid his credibility baggage, or ask the state to appeal Lunden's ruling suppressing the evidence and see where it takes us. To wait on the Court of Appeals to decide a case for the prosecution when the odds of winning are overwhelmingly against them is not justified. We may be talking years of delay, and our momentum in pursuing our investigation would come to a halt. Neither of the options are justified, so we will call in Sands and see how he performs. Only after an interview can we best assess his usage. Of course, that decision may depend on other investigative developments at the time we need to decide on Sands. For now, that is how we will proceed." ⚖️

The presidential election of November 1980 resulted in a new president taking office from a different political party than the one that had held the office. Consequently, the Attorney General, Solomon Gold, was newly appointed. His background included primarily civil cases in nature; he was not known as a litigator and had no prior experience in criminal law. Attorney General Gold was a close friend of the newly elected president and a substantial contributor to his campaign. Gold had a neutral reputation on crime matters. He was not a conservative who professed being tough on crime or a bleeding heart liberal who tended to eschew personal responsibility for those committing criminal acts.

Although the prior Attorney General had generally approved the use of fabricated cases to be presented to judges suspected of corruption, with the consequence that undercover FBI agents and undercover lawyers representing them could, among other things, lie to the judges and others in presenting their cases, newly appointed Attorney General Gold called for a meeting in Washington, D.C. to discuss the propriety and legality of this method of investigation to be employed in Operation Greylord.

Prior to the meeting in Washington, D.C. at the Department of Justice, the U.S. Attorney in Chicago called a meeting with his top people and the FBI Special Agent in Charge in Chicago to go over plans for the meeting. Attendees at the Chicago meeting were the following: U.S. Attorney Brandon Hartnett, First Assistant U.S. Attorney Ben Jones, Assistant U.S. Attorney Dan Hogan, Assistant State's Attorney Peter Theos, and FBI Special Agent in Charge of the Chicago office Harry Meredith.

Hartnett addressed the gathering, "Good morning, gentlemen. I assume most of you got this correspondence from the newly appointed Attorney General of the Department of Justice, but just in case, I sent each of you a copy yesterday. In case you haven't had a chance to see it, let me read it to you."

Hartnett then read the following:

"Dear United States Attorney Hartnett:
Although it had been my desire to travel to U.S. Attorneys' offices in the major cities to meet officials there early in my tenure as Attorney General, a matter has come to my attention which requires my immediate attention and which has necessitated a meeting in my office at the earliest possible time. I apologize for not having met you and your staff in the normal routine of business, but I believe that the investigation styled "Operation Greylord" presents certain aspects which appear to be troublesome.

"With apologies for the urgency of the meeting, I ask that you and your relevant staff meet with me and others in my office a week from today at 10 A.M. I look forward to meeting you then.

Solomon Gold
Attorney General of the United States"

"I would like to hear your reactions to his observations and how you think we should respond," said Hartnett to the group.

Hogan spoke first, "Well, I don't think it's good news. He must be aware that his predecessor approved of the investigation and the methods involved, but he is sure stifling his enthusiasm about the project. It seems he has a different view of its importance and how to go about gaining evidence. It sure would help if he had even a little bit of background in criminal law and an idea of the cesspool of corruption we're looking into."

"I agree with Dan. The A.G. must know that the Bureau is on board with it, and what we've done so far sure looks like we're on the money with our suspicions. You know, Abscam left a sour taste in a lot of people's mouths. I hate to admit that investigating a bunch of congressmen, making up a goofy scenario, and not finding any real crime—just our fictitious stuff—made us all look bad. But everyone in this room knows this investigation is a lot different than Abscam, and we're making headway with real corruption involving bad judges," Meredith said.

Jones added, "Besides the bad outcome the Government had with Abscam, a political cynic might say that a reason to end the inquiry is because the prior administration started it. There's no reason for me to think the new A.G. is a political creature, but I'm sure he wants to protect the President from unnecessary political risk. And we all have to admit, there is some risk involved here. Illinois was a key state that went for the president in the election, and to jump on some of its bigwigs with charges of corruption early in his tenure is not the way to go about keeping friends and influencing people. It takes some balls to approve federal FBI agents lying to state court judges to see if they're crooked or not. They may not feel bound to continue our probe unless we can make the case that there is a strong basis to continue and that lying to corrupt judges was necessitated by the circumstances."

Hartnett then said, "We will soon know what the new administration is thinking, but one thing we can all agree on is the need to make a compelling case that judicial corruption has to be eradicated at all costs and that our results so far justify our continuation of what we are doing, at least on an incremental basis. Helpful to our position is the fact that there have been no leaks of any kind, so we have been spared rampant public speculation about what we are doing and why we are doing it. I would like each of you to prepare a brief position paper for me to review so as to guide us in our meeting next week in Washington and to put the best possible face on what we're doing and why. Get that to me as soon as possible. Thank you all for coming. I want each of you to be part of the group when we meet the A.G. and his staff next week. I don't have to tell you that it's a make-or-break meeting."

As requested, the Chicago contingent engaged in Operation Greylord flew to Washington D.C. to the Department of Justice Building. The meeting room was very ornate with a rich long table, plush chairs, and paintings of prior Attorneys General on the wall. The room oozed formality, dignity and history.

The high offices and stature of the attendees was in harmony with the majesty of the room. The tawdry subject matter of the meeting—crooked judges who take money to fix cases—and its contrast to the setting was not lost on the participants.

Attendees for the Department of Justice were: Attorney General Solomon Gold, Deputy Attorney General William O'Brien, and FBI Director Josh Dillon.

Attendees for the U.S. Attorney's Office in Chicago were: U.S. Attorney, Brandon Hartnett, First Assistant U.S. Attorney Ben Jones, Assistant U.S. Attorney in charge of Greylord Dan Hogan, Assistant State's Attorney Peter Theos, and FBI Special Agent in Charge in Chicago, Harry Meredith.

The Attorney General spoke first. "Good morning, everybody. I want to thank you all for coming, particularly the Chicago contingent, on such short notice. As you no doubt guessed from the notice and the subject of the meeting I described for you, I consider the matter to be of the highest priority. I know the project has received a green light from my predecessor, in consultation with FBI Director Dillon, but it is my obligation to determine whether, and to what extent, the investigation should continue. Although these are discretionary matters—I do not see a national security consideration in the project—I recognize what we investigate and how we do so have their own importance to the governance of our country and its effect on our citizens. Let me also say, especially to those who have never met or dealt with me, I value candor in discussions. The fact we are not all equal in the offices we hold does not govern or dictate the depth of your knowledge or the quality of your contribution to the discussion. Perhaps we can start by going around the table and having each participant introduce themselves and the positions they occupy."

Accordingly everybody went around the table and introduced themselves and their offices.

Gold continued, "It seems logical at this point to have U.S. Attorney Hartnett describe the origin of the investigation—Operation Greylord, I understand it's called—its progress to-date and the methods employed."

U.S. Attorney Hartnett then spoke. "Thank you Mr. Attorney General. The very first piece of information we received that institutionalized corruption existed in the Circuit Court of Cook County among some of the judges hearing criminal cases came from a criminal defense lawyer who regularly practiced in that court. That attorney was himself under criminal investigation by my office and, as sometimes occurs, sought to help himself out of his own problems by offering to tell us what he knew about judges on the take. There has always been a sense, developed through the years on bits and pieces of information, case outcomes, and unsubstantiated hearsay, that things in state court—the county courts being part of the state system and referred to as state courts—were not always operating on the up and up. Some cases and results just did not pass the smell test. For example, there was a long tenured judge—part of a politically connected family—who sat in criminal court. As you know, Mr. Attorney General, every criminal defendant charged with felony violations is entitled to a trial by jury. Interestingly enough, the prosecution does not have that same right. If a criminal defendant waives his right to a jury, the trial will be a bench trial. The judge presiding will be the fact finder and the state's attorney cannot do a thing about it. This particular judge only had bench trials—virtually no defendant ever took a jury trial when he was the assigned judge. For years, every elected State's Attorney in Cook County, as well as others in the state, would lobby the legislature in Springfield to pass legislation that would give the State's Attorneys the same right to trial by jury that defendants had. It never happened. So how do you think all those bench trials before that judge came out? Either all, or most, were not guilty verdicts. Now I will concede that this particular judge may have been philosophically or morally inclined toward leniency as opposed to some other reason to consistently rule the way he did other than getting bribed, but it sure looked funny. Statistically speaking, those outcomes were indefensible. In the federal system, the prosecutor has to agree to a criminal defendant's waiver of his right to trial by jury. By withholding his consent, the U.S. Attorney can veto the defendant's jury waiver. The bottom line is that the federal prosecutor also has the right to trial by jury and not just the criminal defendant; not so in the state system."

O'Brien asked, "Doesn't the circumstance you paint speak more to the manner of how judges get selected as opposed to their conduct while on the bench?"

Hartnett responded, "I concede that the selection of judges and how that is done would be a starting point in improving the judicial system, but since politics are so entrenched as a method of getting on the bench in Illinois, any other way to improve the system should not be overlooked. If I may, I will call on Dan Hogan to elaborate on the commencement of the investigation and to summarize our actions to date. Let me assure you at the outset that the only similarity between Greylord and the now discredited Abscam investigation is the use of undercover operatives. We are going after real crooked judges here, not just those reacting only to governmental inducements."

By all means, we would like to hear from Mr. Hogan," invited Gold.

"Thank you for the opportunity to speak. Let me first tell you why, of all the cases I have been involved in my years as an Assistant United States Attorney, none has personally inflamed me as much as this one. I recognize we must never act out of anger, but so long as our actions are reasonable and necessary to our mission, recognizing a deep personal distaste for conduct which so broadly affects the rights of ordinary citizens in a direct and profound way is necessary and appropriate. I do not mean to sermonize, especially to this group, but respect for and adherence to the rule of law, which we have all devoted our lives to, is the underpinning for our entire system of government. It is the judicial branch of government, I submit, that touches the lives of our people in the most direct and frequent way. If there is no integrity and fairness in how we resolve civil disputes and determine and punish those who transgress our criminal laws, then we stigmatize society in all of its aspects, and diminish the faith of our citizens in all of our governmental institutions. Mr. Attorney General, you asked for candor and I have offered it to you, including the personal feelings."

"I respect your feelings and am in full agreement with your perspectives. What have you done so far?" asked Gold.

"As mentioned, we were able to debrief a veteran criminal defense lawyer who has practiced almost exclusively in the state courts. He does mostly criminal cases but, on occasion, some civil stuff. He has appeared before just about every judge who handles criminal matters and some who do civil stuff. The essence of what he told us is that certain judges will take money and give favorable rulings in return, both in criminal and civil cases. He also said that in some courts— including traffic court—the practice is institutionalized by some judges and certain lawyers. In a limited number of cases this lawyer handled, we were able to secure some files which tended to corroborate what he was telling us. In addition to that lawyer, we have been able to establish, beyond any doubt, that a large bribe was paid by a lawyer to fix a significant drug case to suppress evidence seized in a car search case. We have invited Peter Theos to be with us today because he can tell you about that case and his own experiences as an Assistant State's Attorney. May he address you?"

"By all means."

Theos addressed the group, "First, let me thank you for permitting me to speak. If you will indulge me a moment, I would like to give you a brief background as to how I got here today. It was through my immigrant parents that I came to love the law. I also wanted to be like them because they were so special and had experienced lawless societies in World War II. I was determined to both honor them and devote my life to the rule of law. My schooling was geared to becoming a lawyer and then to be a prosecutor. I did well in school and finished high up in my law school class. I applied for a job as a prosecutor in Chicago. I got the job of my dreams and got hired as an Assistant State's Attorney in Cook County. I managed to get assigned to the Criminal Division and started right in. Under the system at the States Attorney's office, you are rotated among the various criminal courts and get trained by appearing before a lot of judges. Once training is finished, you get assigned to a courtroom. Judges rotate into that courtroom from time to time, although a particular judge is usually assigned there more than any other judge. I became sickened over what I was seeing take place and just couldn't take it anymore. I saw cases decided, not on the basis of the evidence presented and the governing law, but for reasons I could not understand. Sometimes no reasons were expressed for a decision by the judge. Although I did not have a lot of experience in the courtroom, I had enough to know when things were not right. The final straw was when I was defending the legality of a search of a car and the seizure of a large quantity of drugs. I had two honest cops who had a justifiable reason for stopping a car for a traffic violation, summoning a police dog to sniff the car and alerting to drugs and, along with other circumstances, finding and seizing two kilos of cocaine from a hidden compartment in the car. Everything was done by the book, the actions of the police were corroborated and, under the prevailing law, the seizure was lawful. After the testimony of both police officers and other evidence was presented, the defendant got up on the stand and testified to a different version of events—he basically called the cops liars, even though the defendant's version was neither reasonable nor corroborated. Now I know I am an advocate, but I never lost my objectivity. After the evidence was presented by both sides, the judge recessed the hearing. In about one week, he issued a very brief opinion with hardly any analysis. All he said was that the defendant's version of the events was more consistent with his real-life experiences, was more credible than the testimony of the two police officers, and that the defendant's constitutional rights were violated. That was it. Just like that. He ignored the fact that the defendant had two prior felony convictions for drug dealing and, under the law, the judge could consider those convictions as bearing on the believability of the defendant. The judge didn't say boo about those convictions, as if they didn't matter. And that is what I came to believe; those convictions did not matter because the case was wired. And you know what really stinks?

We cannot appeal that ruling to a higher court because the judge predicated his ruling on the credibility of witnesses; a trial judge's discretion as to who to believe is essentially non-reviewable. The case law is uniform that the fact finder—here, the judge—who hears the witnesses is in the best position to determine which witnesses are worthy of belief—end of story. Since we cannot introduce the drugs in evidence, we have no case. I knew in my heart and mind that the ruling was not the product of the facts, law, or the judge's experiences of life. I did not know what to do, and my revulsion at what just happened would not go away."

After a short pause, Theos continued, "And then a funny thing happened. I got a phone call from Dan Hogan. He was cryptic in the call, told me who he was, and said he would like to see me. He didn't say about what, and I did not ask. We arranged to meet. I agreed because I was intrigued about the call and Hogan's position as a prosecutor. Dan and I met. In summary, he told me that his office had started an investigation involving judicial corruption in the state court system and had heard about me. He didn't say what he had heard, but alluded to some possible disillusions I may have expressed. I don't know what I may have said to someone in passing, but Hogan sure had it right. I was sickened by what I was seeing, particularly the last drug case I told you about. I knew instinctively I could trust Hogan and, although he could not share details about his investigation, we shared similar views about what may be going on in some state courtrooms. I decided to unload to him about the drug case and told him my suspicion that the judge had been bribed by somebody. I told him that if my suspicions were true, it could only have been the defense lawyer who arranged and executed the transaction. No judge in his right mind would have dealt with the defendant or anyone else directly. It could only have been the lawyer, and the judge and lawyer had known each other through other court appearances."

Theos looked around the room to gauge the effect his words had on the assemblage. "Hogan told me he would give some thought to the drug case and that he would call me. He asked me what I thought he could do. I told him since we had no hard evidence of a bribe, he would have nothing to lose by subpoenaing the lawyer to appear before the grand jury, bestowing immunity on him, and then forcing him to testify. If he denied a bribe, at least we would have his denial under oath. If evidence was later developed that there was a bribe, the lawyer could be charged with perjury before the grand jury. On the other hand, if he testified that a bribe was in fact involved, then we would have something to go against the judge. Even though the lawyer got immunity and could not be prosecuted for bribery based on his grand jury testimony, the more important target of prosecution was the judge and the gamble of using immunity to secure the testimony would have been well worthwhile. Hogan promised we would meet again soon."

At that point, Gold interrupted. "And did that in fact occur?"

"Sure enough we met again within a week. Hogan said he liked my idea of immunity for the lawyer. I was thrilled because my feelings were strong that it would prove productive. Sometime later, Hogan got approval to give the lawyer immunity. He put the lawyer in the grand jury, who sang the words to the tune of my belief. He did bribe that judge. Hogan now had a strong basis to indict the judge after a little more necessary investigation to corroborate what really happened. Dan Hogan and I then had discussions about my joining the effort to uncover even more judicial corruption. I was enthused about doing so. We developed a plan where I would, at some point, leave the State's Attorney's office, hang out a shingle as a newly minted criminal defense lawyer, and start portraying myself as a zealous defense lawyer willing to do anything necessary to win cases and get my clients off the hook, that is, the kind of crooked lawyer I despised. In that role, I would gather evidence about corruption at various levels from judges on down, including lawyers, clerks, and police officers."

Hogan then interjected, "At the risk of embarrassing Peter, let me say we have never worked with a more dedicated individual nor one who has produced such important information."

Attorney General Gold then said, "I think what you have done so far is both productive and justifiable. We regularly use immunity that way, when we have a basis to do so. But it is my understanding that your office has developed a protocol to follow in other cases which may be problematic, if not downright improper. What I am referring to are circumstances in which our undercover FBI agents who are lawyers are appearing before state court judges who are targets of the investigation. These undercover lawyers then lie to the judges—and other court officials—on a regular basis during the pendency of the cases they are appearing on. I am troubled about that for these reasons. In the Abscam investigation with which you are all no doubt familiar, our agents lied to duly elected Congressional legislators and other high government officials in order to snare them if they acted improperly. You all know how Abscam turned out. Our techniques of fabricated scenarios and lies made to the targets were highly criticized by many respected commentators when the investigation ended. More importantly, hardly anyone took our bait and got convicted of any federal violations so, when all was said and done, the FBI and the Department of Justice had egg all over their faces. They spent a lot of money to do the Abscam investigation and used up a lot of political capital and goodwill in having the executive branch of government investigate the legislative branch of government. Worse yet, they had virtually no results that would have justified what was done. The key features of Abscam, fabricated scenarios and lies to suspected officials who are the targets, seem to be repeating themselves here. As a newly installed administration, it seems unwise to reengage in conduct by DOJ and the FBI which may represent the lowest points in their respective history."

After a sip of water, Gold continued, "As the Chief Law Enforcement officer of the United States, I am not anxious to start off my tenure by authorizing practices which not only have failed in the past, but well may be illegal. It is one thing for an undercover FBI agent to lie to a Congressman, it is another thing for a licensed attorney, subject to a code of ethics, lying to a state court judge as a routine matter. I do not believe any state's rules of ethics governing lawyer conduct permits lies to be told to judges, in court, in the interests of a criminal investigation to ferret out judicial corruption."

Hartnett took the floor. "Mr. Attorney General, let me first off say that the manner of how to investigate what we strongly believe to be rampant judicial corruption in Cook County has been the subject of hours of discussion in my office by relevant officials and, as you know, include your predecessor and his staff. I do not mean to suggest that, by virtue of his prior approval, all of the risks in this form of investigation have disappeared or that you are somehow bound to maintain his prior authorization to proceed in the way we have. Let me emphasize for you and your staff what we believe justifies what we have done so far and what we would like to continue doing. First off, every licensed attorney in Illinois who is participating in the Greylord investigation, whether appearing personally before a state court judge and lying to him or not, runs the risk of the loss of his or her license to practice law. There is no exception in our rule of ethics which permits lying to a judge, or abetting the lie while acting in a legal capacity. Good faith exceptions for law enforcement officers acting altruistically do not exist. We all know the risk and, before anyone signs up to work on Greylord, the risk is fully explained. Let me also explain how we settled on creating made-up or fabricated cases, involving only undercover FBI agents acting as participants to phony accidents, and phony altercations with undercover FBI lawyers representing them in court. The alternative method to doing the investigation would be to examine historical documents and put witnesses in the grand jury, with or without immunity as circumstances dictate, and see where that leads us. The fundamental defect of the historical method of investigation is that we could not control the secrecy of the investigation. As soon as word leaked about what we were doing, and it inevitably would, evidence would disappear, and witnesses would clam up. We would have to dish out immunity by the truckload, and the likelihood of uncovering most, if not all, of the judicial corruption taking place would be non-existent. We settled on the phony scenario method of getting before the target judges and developing evidence accordingly. We have, however, put in some safeguards. It would be foolish, and probably self-defeating, to target judges randomly. Before we ever try to develop a phony case before a judge, we have to have some evidence, whether direct or circumstantial, that the judge was, in the language of our profession, more likely than not to be corrupt. Similar to the two *Washington Post* reporters writing about Watergate, they had to have two sources of information they considered credible before they would print something. In our case, we determine the credibility of information we have before we set our sights on someone. The drug case we described earlier is an example of that. In Illinois and elsewhere, it is not an unusual law enforcement technique for an undercover agent to lie to a suspected law violator. Drug cases are commonly made when an undercover law enforcement agent acts as an apparent buyer or seller of drugs when dealing with suspects or targets. Similarly, some of our best official governmental corruption cases have been made with undercover agents offering to pay bribes for the performance of illegal acts or to receive them, pretending to be corrupt officials. The notion of this kind of deception used by law enforcement people is well established and approved as a lawful enforcement tool. If we did not fabricate cases to get before a judge believed to be corrupt in order to develop good evidence, the only other way to get before that judge would be to use real cases as our tool. The obvious problem with that is real criminal defendants might wind up getting acquitted. Securing real and proper justice in such cases would be defeated, and the consequence of that real criminal defendant committing future crimes is too big a risk. The other legal principle our office relied on to safeguard the prosecution and conviction of someone not otherwise inclined to act corruptly is the doctrine of entrapment. Anybody on our side dealing directly or indirectly with a suspect judge was carefully instructed to refrain from inducing a judge to take an illegal payment. The law permits us to create the opportunity for one disposed to act corruptly to do so, but not to entice them in such a way as to overcome any initial unwillingness to violate the law. We know where to draw the line, and the experiences of Abscam have not been lost on us. We have all recognized the risks to us individually in how we go about the investigation, taken great care to put safeguards in place to trap only the unwary who are disposed to act corruptly and leave the honest judges alone. After all, it is the honest ones who are tarnished by the corrupt ones, aside from the enormous harm judicial corruption inflicts on the citizens of our country. Corrupt judges are an invidious lot, and we believe they must be exposed and punished for their acts. We do not believe our methods trample on their Constitutional rights and the evidence developed so far—the details of which are reflected in the reports delivered prior to this meeting—is compelling. The corruption is widespread and infects many levels of our system of criminal and civil justice."

"Mr. O'Brien, is there anything you would like to ask of our Chicago visitors at this time?" asked Attorney General Gold.

O'Brien responded, "No thank you. I think the issues have been ably expressed and thoroughly discussed."

"Mr. Director, your agency is doing a lot of the heavy lifting here. You and your agents have been involved from the beginning. Do you have any hesitation about continuing as you have?" asked Gold.

Dillon responded, "I not only have no hesitation in proceeding with Greylord, I am looking forward to it, as are my people. The risks discussed this morning have concentrated on legal policies, fairness, methods, and law licenses. We agree with everything that has been done so far, but I want to address another risk not discussed, but just as important, and perhaps more so, in certain instances. These concocted scenarios have and will continue to involve our special agents pretending to commit certain crimes and other violations. They are brought before judges who will have to decide whether to set bond and, if so, in what amount. There are circumstances where some of my people have been and will be incarcerated for a period, short or perhaps long and overnight. In those cases, the risks are twofold. One is that they will be in the midst of some people who have committed real crimes, and some of the serious variety. The physical safety of our agents can neither be assured nor insured. These are real possibilities. The second potential risk is that Chicago Police or other law enforcement officers, some of whom may themselves be targets in the Greylord investigation, may become suspicious of the true identities and purposes of our special agents. These possibilities are not merely fanciful. Although we are certainly aware of the need for the fictitious identities to be foolproof, the undercover roles do not come with guarantees. All these risks have been thoroughly explained to our people involved. To a person, they have looked forward to participating. Nobody has declined."

Gold reacted, "I am heartened by their willingness to participate, but am not surprised by their enthusiasm."

Dillon continued, "From what I have seen so far, we are achieving a good deal of success. The suspicions have, in some significant cases, proved out. The caliber of agents and attorneys couldn't be higher and, at our bureau, on a voluntary basis. We have had to turn away some agents because of the sheer numbers of volunteers. Mr. Attorney General, I have lived through the failures of Abscam, even if only as a special agent. I offer you professional expertise that Greylord involves real corruption by judges. Our phony cases are but a stepping stone directly to the suspect judge and, for that reason, fully justified. None of us can avoid blemishes to our reputations should we fail in our mission, but that is the reality of the professions we have chosen. As Director of the FBI, I not only accept the risks of Operation Greylord as my duty, I do so with full confidence in its ultimate success. The least we can do as public servants is restore faith to the "rule of law" and its proper place in our system of justice."

Gold then said, "Director Dillon, you enjoy a reputation for integrity and ability. Now that we have met, the attribute of "eloquence" shall be added to your resume. On behalf of my staff, I want to thank the Chicago contingent for coming here to meet on a topic of the highest importance. My staff and I will meet tomorrow morning and discuss these issues. You will have my final decision about proceeding with Operation Greylord before the week is out."

Three days later, Attorney General Solomon Gold sent a coded email to Brandon Hartnett—Re Operation Greylord: Full Speed Ahead. ⚖

Having received the endorsement from Attorney General Solomon Gold to proceed full bore with Operation Greylord, plans were made to move Peter Theos into an active drug courtroom as the assigned first chair prosecutor. The plan was for Theos to commence the reputation as an Assistant State's Attorney who, after conducting himself as a squeaky clean prosecutor all of his career, was now inclined to be friendlier to criminal defense lawyers and more sympathetic to the positions and requests of the defense lawyers and their clients.

Theos' courtroom assignment was to be with Judge Sam Wilson and, of course, to become friendly with the judge and ingratiate himself with the regular defense lawyers who appeared before Judge Wilson. Wilson's was a high-volume courtroom with many preliminary hearings, bond settings and other pretrial matters conducted regularly. Dozens of cases were heard each day, many of a routine nature. As a general rule, court reporters were only assigned to record trials or hearings on motions to suppress, with the host of other matters not recorded for future use.

Although the appearances by defendants and the lawyers before the judge were formal in nature, other contacts between prosecutors, defense counsel, and the judge were markedly informal. Nobody would have raised an eyebrow of suspicion if a defense lawyer or prosecutor sauntered into the judge's chambers, whether alone or together, prior to scheduled sessions to share a cup of coffee and exchange greetings and the day's gossip.

Open-door policies were long the tradition for Judge Wilson. He enjoyed the banter that always accompanied such visits and, indeed, encouraged them. The rule against ex parte discussions between a lawyer and a judge was taken to apply strictly to conversations about cases pending before the judge in which the lawyers were involved and not to contacts generally. Even the rule against ex parte contacts was, to say the least, liberally interpreted.

Judge Sam Wilson was the proverbial hail fellow well met. Theos went to his chambers early on the day of his first assignment to Wilson's courtroom. Theos was tinged with excitement, but also experienced a mild case of nerves. Because of Wilson's reputation as a free-wheeling judge, Theos knew the importance of the first meeting and Act One of his newly adopted charade in his undercover role. Any success Greylord may achieve, Theos knew, would depend in large part on his performance as an actor. The stakes were high with Wilson, even if known only to Theos.

As Theos knocked on Judge Wilson's chambers door and was invited to enter, the conversation ensued. "Good morning, Judge. My name is Peter Theos. It looks like we'll be seeing a lot of each other because I was just assigned to your courtroom as first chair."

"Good morning, Peter. Glad to have you. I take it you've had a little experience in this building already, and maybe even worked some drug cases before. That's all we hear in this room; mostly pretrial stuff along with hearings on motions to suppress and that sort of thing. We also try some cases from time to time, both jury and bench, but the majority of the stuff are pretrial matters."

"That's fine with me, and I'm looking forward to it. You have a great reputation for moving cases along, and I like to keep busy."

"We're going to be busy all right, and you will get your fill of it."

"Do you have a public defender assigned to the courtroom? Are there a lot of appointed cases, or is it mostly defendants who have their own retained lawyers?"

"We have a bit of everything, but more appointments from me than privately retained ones. We always have a public defender, but they rotate a lot. None stay long enough to get known. We also have the Chicago Bar Association representatives, but they also rotate a lot and are not always here. Because of the heavy volume we carry, I often have to appoint lawyers in cases that I know from past experience just to move cases along. In those appointments, the lawyers can make their own deals for payments of fees. They usually work for the CBRs that defendants have coming, so it works out real well."

"Thanks for the tutorial, Judge. I should get the hang of it quickly because I don't want to slow you down. I know the volume of cases is off the charts, and I too want them to move."

"I'm sure you won't, Peter. I look forward to working with you."

"Thank you very much, Judge."

Shortly after assuming his duties as first chair in Judge Wilson's courtroom, Peter Theos was approached by criminal defense lawyer Roger Flynn. Although he had never met Flynn before, Theos knew Flynn was one of the regular practitioners before Wilson and was assigned to a high volume of unrepresented drug defendants by Wilson. As such, Flynn's income was greatly affected by the Wilson-Flynn relationship.

"Hey, how ya doin? I'm Roger Flynn, and one of my cases is up today."

"Fine, how are you? I'm Peter Theos and I was recently assigned to Judge Wilson's courtroom as first chair prosecutor."

"Nice to meet you. You been in the office awhile? I don't think we've ever met."

"No, I don't think we have met. I've been an ASA for a couple of years, but have spent most of my time over in Traffic Court or in the Branch Courts. This is the first permanent assignment here at 26th and California, and I'm hoping to stay awhile."

"No reason why you shouldn't, especially in Wilson's court. It is one of two high volume drug courts and, although you won't get any trials here, you'll have a lot of action. Lots of hearings, motions to suppress, that kind of stuff. And Wilson likes to keep things moving."

"Yeah, that's what he told me. He seems to be a really nice guy and I guess he works like hell to keep everything moving."

"Sam is a great guy and does work hard. He's got his own procedures to keep things moving. He's got a P.D. around, and a CBA guy is often here for handling indigent cases or where the defendant is not represented. A few of us defense lawyers—guys he knows and trusts to do things right—get appointed by him from time to time. Those appointments help us pay the rent and, if worst comes to worst, he'll assign us to the CBR—Cash Bond Refund—as our fee payment. The CBRs are not a lot, but they add up because of the volume, so it pays to stay on Judge Wilson's good side. You'll find out he's really a nice guy, although as an ASA you might think he's a little soft every once in a while. But he knows you just can't throw everyone in jail all the time, and he takes a lot of things into consideration when he makes his rulings."

Theos, adopting an understanding attitude, said, "I think I know what you mean. He probably has to make a lot of close calls, and maybe the guy in front of him is a young guy, bad home life, etc., etc. Some of these guys don't get a fair shake when they start out in life—I understand."

"You're right. A lot of them are young, no father at home, mother is working, and they only answer to a grandmother, when they bother to answer at all. They wind up out in the street all the time. The gangs are everywhere, and drugs are the coin of the realm in the neighborhood. What real choices do these guys have? We're all supposed to walk the straight and narrow, but out where they live, none of the streets are straight, even when they are narrow. Not too many choices for these guys, and most of them are bad choices. A judge like Wilson understands that, and sometimes cuts some defendants a little slack even if it is not exactly by the book."

Theos, in a spirit of sympathy said, "I see what you mean."

"Sam does not have a by the book reputation. He often goes by his instincts and his heart, and if you keep that in mind, you'll be able to understand why he does some of the things he does instead of wearing blinders and looking only at conduct and not at all the circumstances. You'll never hear anybody call him a hanging judge because he isn't. But he sure has a big heart."

Theos under his breath murmured to himself "and a big wallet." Then he asked Flynn, "Have you got something up today?"

"I had a small marijuana case but the judge thought it was such a small case he thought you would nolle it. I'm sure he'll talk to you about it, but he thought for sure you would agree with him so he sent me on my way."

"If it wasn't a big deal to the judge, I'm sure it would not be a big deal to me."

Flynn, nodding with approval, said, "I'm sure he'll be happy to hear you say that. That's one of the ways he keeps things moving around here, especially the small stuff."

"No problem. But will you get paid on the case if it's not even called in open court and dismissed on the record?"

"Sure thing. I got the CBR the kid put up—the bond was $10,000 and he put up 10%, or $1,000. The CBR is good for the thou, other than some minor processing costs for the clerk's office. We all saved some time in this case by the judge's dismissal, but you and I—especially me—got paid just the same. You all right with that?"

"Not a problem. It's a good way to move the docket," lied Theos.

"Great. I look forward to working with you in court."

"Me too. Take care." ⚖

After a couple of days handling some routine matters, Peter Theos was working at his desk when Roger Flynn stuck his head into Theos's office early one morning. Theos had been preparing for a hearing on a Motion to Suppress Evidence filed by Flynn prior to Theos's assignment to Judge Wilson's courtroom; the hearing was scheduled for that morning.

"Well, how ya doing, Peter," asked Flynn.

"Not too bad, but I have a little problem this morning because one of my two police officers has not shown up yet for the hearing and I don't want to go with just one," responded Theos.

"I don't want to fight you on this one, Peter, but my guy took a day off work to be here and he's like a cat on a hot tin roof. A continuance is going to cost him more money, and I don't think he is up to it. Besides, if you have one of the coppers, what difference does it make?"

Theos responded, "Two is always better than one and it just makes my position that much stronger."

"I was going to ask you this anyway, so if you agree, it will only be your guy and just a brief stipulation as what my client would testify to. I'd rather not put him on the stand and, if you stipulate, it will only be your man live against my client's stipulation as to what he would say. The judge will not actually hear directly from him. What do you say, Peter?"

Peter responded as follows, "I will stipulate as you ask, that's not a problem. But I still would rather have both my officers here so I am going to ask the judge to put it over."

"Peter, I understand your position but, just so you know, I'm going to object. But I want to know if you will still stipulate in case the judge does not grant your request for a continuance. My guy is anxious to go forward."

"Roger, I will stipulate as I said I would, whatever way the judge goes on my request. Don't worry about that."

"Peter, I like dealing with you since you keep your word when you give it. Not everybody does that."

"Roger, you don't have to worry about me. I say what I mean and mean what I say. Let's go to court."

"I'm right behind you, Peter."

Shaking hands as they left the office and entered the courtroom, Louis Toms, the court clerk, called the court back into session. Judge Sam Wilson was on the bench.

The transcript of the morning's events reflects the following:

Toms: Court is back in session; please come to order. Case of State versus Tripp, 78CR319. Hearing on defendant's motion to suppress evidence. Counsel and all others present please state your name and your office.

Theos: Good morning, Your Honor, Peter Theos for the state. With me is Chicago police officer George Spangler, one of the two arresting officers.

Flynn: Good morning, Your Honor. I'm Roger Flynn, counsel for the defendant Amos Tripp, who is present.

Wilson: Well, is everyone ready to go? How many witnesses will be testifying this morning?

Theos: As a matter of fact, Your Honor, the State is requesting a short continuance in this case. Although one of the two arresting officers is present and ready to testify, the second arresting officer, although scheduled to be here and to testify, is not here and we don't know where he is.

Flynn: Judge, the defendant objects to any continuance. This hearing was set by Your Honor over one month ago for everyone's convenience. My client has taken a day off of work in order to be here. The State has a witness here ready to testify and, presumably, can testify to everything the absent officer would have testified to. For the Court and the rest of us to be inconvenienced to accommodate an absent witness who apparently hasn't even bothered to call the Assistant State's Attorney to explain his absence is both unnecessary and unjustified. I strongly object to the motion for a continuance.

Theos: Your Honor, I recognize the predicament I have been put in by our missing officer and I cannot offer an explanation for his absence. We don't know whether something has occurred, beyond his ability to overcome, that prevents his appearance. God forbid that nothing bad has happened to him or a loved one, and it is not appropriate to speculate why he is not here. It is possible he may offer testimony which would not be presented by Officer Spangler but, even if he did not, his testimony would almost certainly be helpful in the Court's determination of the credibility of witnesses. Nobody else was in the defendant's car, so a complete record of what happened out there would call for testimony of all three witnesses. To be somewhat inconvenient to all I will concede, but there is nothing urgent requiring dispatch. As for the defendant's missing work today, the State will reimburse him for any lost wages he may suffer.

Wilson: I understand that none of this is your fault, Mr. Theos, but I am not persuaded it is necessary to hear from two witnesses on your side since nobody, including you, has asserted that Officer Spangler does not know and cannot convey the entirety of the matters observed and heard when the defendant's car was stopped by the police that day. Add to that the fact that everyone agreed that today was best for all parties and witnesses to be present, and we have no word of explanation to measure why we should continue the hearing. I am confident that I will have a full record of relevant evidence on which to base my ruling on the motion to suppress. For these reasons, I deny the motion to continue the suppression hearing. The State may call its witness.

Toms: Mr. Witness, will you please stand and raise your right hand: Do you solemnly swear that the testimony you give on the hearing before this Court shall be the truth, the whole truth, and nothing but the truth, so help you God?

Spangler: I do.

Theos: Will you please state and spell your full name?

Spangler: George Spangler. G-E-O-R-G-E S-P-A-N-G-L-E-R

Theos: How are you employed?

Spangler: I am a Chicago police officer.

Theos: How long have you been so employed?

Spangler: Six years.

Theos: What is your current assignment with the Chicago Police Department?

Spangler: I am a patrol officer.

Theos: Were you on duty as a patrol officer on May 20, 1977?

Spangler: Yes.

Theos: What were your duty hours that day?

Spangler: 9 a.m. to 6 p.m.

Theos: Directing your attention to about 3 p.m., where were you?

Spangler: We were in the area of 16th and Kenton that afternoon.

Theos: Did you have a partner in your car at that time?

Spangler: Yes.

Theos: What was your partner's name?

Spangler: Andy Tribble.

Theos: Who was driving?

Spangler: I was.

Theos: Did you and Officer Tribble conduct a traffic stop at that time and place?

Spangler: Yes.

Theos: What car did you stop?

Spangler: The defendant's car; a 1976 four door black Buick.

Theos: Why did you stop the car?

Spangler: It had a broken taillight.

Theos: Could you see that clearly from the inside of your car?

Spangler: Yes, because we pulled up behind him.

Theos: In what manner did you stop the car?

Spangler: We put on the Mars light and he pulled over right away.

Theos: What happened next?

Spangler: We both got out of our car. I went up to the driver's side door and asked the driver for his driver's license.

Theos: What did your partner do?

Spangler: He went to the passenger's door, and I could see him do a visual inspection of the inside of the car.

Theos: Was anybody else in the car?

Spangler: No.

Theos: What happened next?

Spangler: The driver, who I now know as Amos Tripp, handed me his driver's license. He asked me why he was pulled over.

Theos: What did you say or do?

Spangler: I told him the rear right taillight was broken, and the brake light did not come on when he stopped at the stop sign.

Theos: What did he say to that?

Spangler: He said it could not be; that the car was only two years old and everything was working as far as he knew.

Theos: What happened next?

Spangler: I asked him to get out of the car because he appeared quite nervous while I was talking to him. We were in a neighborhood known to have a high incidence of drug usage among the residents and buyers from the suburbs coming there to buy drugs. I also wanted to show him the tail light.

Theos: Did he get out of the car?

Spangler: Yes, he did. He seemed more nervous than ever and said he did not want to see the tail light then. He said he would check it out later.

Theos: What did you make of his answer?

Spangler: I thought it was unusual to not go back behind the trunk to look at the tail light in light of his statement that the car was fairly new, and he thought everything was working. I started to think he did not want us to go near the trunk.

Theos: What happened next?

Spangler: I asked him why he was acting so nervous around us since it was just a traffic citation. I said if he fixed the light before a court appearance, he could probably beat the ticket.

Theos: Then what happened?

Spangler: As I started to walk back to show him the light and got near the trunk, he appeared even more nervous and started to break out into a sweat. Noticing this, I got suspicious about him and I began to think he had drugs in the car somewhere. So I just asked him directly, "do you have any drugs in the car?"

Theos: What did he say?

Spangler: He said, and I quote, "hell no, man. I'm clean." I told him if he was really clean, he wouldn't object if we searched him.

Theos: What did he say?

Spangler: He said, "Go ahead and search me."

Theos: Then what?

Spangler: My partner and I then searched Amos personally.

Theos: Did you find anything illegal?

Spangler: No, he was clean.

Theos: What happened next?

Spangler: I asked Mr. Tripp if it was all right to search the car, including the locked trunk.

Theos: What did he say to that?

Spangler: He said we wouldn't find anything, and that the trunk was a mess because he had some laundry in there, along with a bunch of other junk. He said it would be a lot of trouble.

Theos: What did you say to that?

Spangler: We told him we didn't mind, but it would clear things up if he let us do it now instead of us trying to get a search warrant for the car from a judge and delaying everything for hours while we did that.

Theos: Did he respond to that?

Spangler: He still seemed nervous, but I could see him thinking about it. He asked whether his car would be tied up for that whole period of time if we did that.

Theos: What did you say?

Spangler: I told him I was afraid so.

Theos: What else did you say?

Spangler: I told him we would hurry and be quick about it, and we wouldn't bother about calling a dog to the scene to sniff for the scent of drugs in the car.

Theos: What did he say then?

Spangler: He asked if we would promise to be quick about it. I assured him it wouldn't take more than 10 minutes. I also told him he didn't have to give us consent to search if he did not want to give it.

Theos: What did he say to that?

Spangler: He said we could search if we would be quick about it.

Theos: Did you ask him to sign a consent to search form formalizing his consent to search the car?

Spangler: No, we didn't. See, we just wanted to hurry and get it over with before he decided to change his mind. Besides, we didn't have any blank consent to search forms in the car, although we usually carry them with us.

Theos: What happened then?

Spangler: We had Mr. Tripp open the trunk first since an eyeball inspection of the interior of the car did not disclose anything out of the ordinary or any indication there were traps built into the interior where drugs could be hidden.

Theos: What was the result of the search of the trunk?

Spangler: Well, he was right. There was all kinds of stuff in the trunk, including a big laundry bag full of clothes. At the very bottom of the bag, covered by a bunch of clothes, we found a package tightly sealed with cellophane wrap and lots of duct tape. It took us a while to cut it open, take a small sample out of it, and field test the substance. The result was a positive test for heroin, but a laboratory analysis was going to be necessary to establish the chemical make-up of the substance. The later lab test confirmed the presence of heroin, and that's why we're here.

Theos: What happened after your discovery of what was presumptively heroin?

Spangler: We arrested Amos Tripp for possession of heroin with intent to distribute. The quantity in the package was too large to be considered solely for personal use or consumption.

Theos: Your honor, I have no further questions of this witness.

Wilson: Thank you counsel. Mr. Flynn, you may cross-examine.

Flynn: Officer Spangler, you and your partner Andy Tribble, have worked together for a number of years, haven't you?

Spangler: Yes. We both came on the force around the same time and we hit it off right from the first pairing on patrol.

Flynn: He's closer to you than a brother, isn't that true?

Spangler: Yes. I've never been closer to anyone else in my life.

Flynn: And it's true, is it not, that every time you have had to testify in court as a police officer, he has testified at the same time?

Spangler: Yes, that's true.

Flynn: And it's also true, I take it, that you don't know where he is right now or why he's not here?

Spangler: Counselor, you are right on both counts.

Flynn: Officer Spangler, let me change topics at this point. I want to ask you about police procedure. You testified to a great deal of detail about an event that took place a number of months ago, didn't you?

Spangler: Yes, that's true.

Flynn: And you probably refreshed your recollection about your version of events by reviewing a police report you and your partner prepared about these very events a day or so after they transpired, didn't you?

Spangler: Yes, that's true.

Flynn: And it's part of your official duties to memorialize what happened—at least the very important facts—by writing them down and submitting the report to your superiors, isn't that also true?

Spangler: Yes, that's true.

Flynn: And these reports are important because you are not expected to remember, well into the future, all that happened on a particular day.

Spangler: Yes, that's right.

Flynn: Accuracy is important, is it not, as to what the report says and what it does not say, isn't that true?

Spangler: Absolutely right.

Flynn: Now I know you're not a lawyer, are you Officer Spangler?

Spangler: No, I'm not.

Flynn: But you are quite familiar with search and seizure law, aren't you?

Spangler: Maybe not as much as you, Counselor, but I have a working knowledge of the law.

Flynn: And that's because you have made lots of searches and seizures through the years, isn't that right?

Spangler: Yes, quite right.

Flynn: And you have testified dozens of times in hearings like this through the years, haven't you?

Spangler: Too many to count.

Flynn: You've heard of the doctrine, "the fruit of the poisonous tree," haven't you?

Spangler: Yes, many times.

Flynn: And in its purest form, that doctrine holds that if the original stop or arrest of a citizen is illegal, anything searched for or seized from a citizen cannot thereafter be used as evidence in a court of law against that citizen, isn't that right?

Spangler: I accept your summarization of the doctrine as law.

Flynn: And it is your testimony here today that the sole reason you stopped my client's car is because one of the taillights on his car was broken, isn't that right?

Spangler: Yes, that's right.

Flynn: Now in reviewing your police report to refresh your recollection as to these events, did you rely on your review to recall why it was you stopped my client's car?

Spangler: Yes, I believe I did.

Flynn: Officer Spangler, I am going to hand you what has been marked Defense Exhibit One and ask you if that is the report you and your partner prepared in this case around the time of the arrest of my client.

Spangler: It sure looks like it.

Flynn: Well, it is, isn't it?

Spangler: Yes.

Flynn: And that is the report you reviewed to refresh your recollection as to the important events in this case?

Spangler: It is.

Flynn: And the most important event in this case is the stop of my client's car and the reason for the stop.

Spangler: Yes, that's fair.

Flynn: I want you to review the entirety of that report and point out for all of us, including the judge, the portion of the report which describes the reason why you and your partner stopped my client's car that day.

The witness studies the report for a prolonged period of time and then hands the report back to defense counsel.

Flynn: Officer Spangler, would you please do what I asked you to do?

Spangler: I can't do it.

Flynn: Why not?

Spangler: Because I don't see that reference in the report.

Flynn: Are you sure? Did you review the report carefully?

Spangler: Yes, I'm sure. I don't see it there.

Flynn: Do you think it's not there because neither you nor your partner wrote it in there?

Spangler: That must be the case. I can think of no other reason it is not in the report.

Flynn: Officer Spangler, I just want to cover one other area briefly with you, and then I'll be finished. When you described to my client the fact that a search warrant could be obtained to search a person's car—you remember that topic, don't you?

Spangler: Yes, I remember it.

Flynn: You not only told my client the procedure involved in getting a search warrant, you also estimated the lengthy amount of time it would take to do so, isn't that right?

Spangler: Right.

Flynn: And you weren't just giving my client a primer on the law of search and seizure, were you?

Spangler: I don't understand. I don't know what you mean.

Flynn: What I mean is this—you told my client that you would go and get a search warrant if he did not consent to a search, didn't you?

Spangler: I'm pretty sure we just told him we would try to get one, not that we would for sure get it.

Flynn: And you told him you would hold him and his car for hours while doing so, isn't that right?

Spangler: We told him that because it's true, we were lawfully permitted to do that.

Flynn: Only if my client was arrested and in custody, isn't that right?

Spangler: I guess so.

Flynn: One last area of inquiry, Officer Spangler, and then you'll be finished. Now you say you didn't have any blank forms for a "Consent to Search," isn't that right?

Spangler: I guess so.

Flynn: You're not really guessing, are you? You know any piece of paper will do, so long as it's signed and it is clear what the paper is for.

Spangler: Right.

Flynn: And you had other paper available to write the simple words, "I consent to a search of my car" with a place for the consenter's signature?

Spangler: I guess we did, but neither of us thought to do it since he gave his oral consent.

Flynn: At least, that's what you contend, isn't it?

Spangler: Yes, that's right.

Flynn: I have no further questions.

Wilson: Mr. Theos, do you have any redirect examination?

Theos: No, Your Honor. I think everything has been covered. The witness may be excused.

Flynn: Your Honor, the prosecutor and I have entered into a brief stipulation to present to you as part of the evidentiary record in this case. He has been good enough to do it this way at my request in order to safeguard my client's Constitutional rights and not be forced to be a witness, even for purposes of this hearing. The stipulation is as follows:

"If called as a witness, Amos Tripp, the defendant in this case, would testify at trial:

1. That at no time on May 20, 1977, either before or after his car stop and later arrest by George Spangler and his partner in or around the intersection of 16th and Kenton on Chicago's west side, did the car he was driving have a broken or inoperable taillight;

2. That a test of the brake lights later that day showed that they worked properly;

3. That he was never asked to give consent to search his car by any officer, either orally or in writing;

4. That he never gave any police officer, either orally or in writing, consent to search his car in any way or at any location."

I ask that you receive and consider this stipulation, in your consideration and determination of my client's Motion to Suppress Evidence. Thank you very much.

Wilson: I will take the motion and the evidence presented under advisement.

The following was a conversation between Prosecutor Peter Theos and Defense Counsel Roger Flynn shortly after the conclusion of the hearing in the empty courtroom. Nobody else was present or privy to the conversation, with the exception that Peter Theos was wearing a wire and the conversation was being recorded. A transcript of the recorded conversation reads as follows:

Flynn: Peter, I appreciate the fact you stipulated to my client's limited, but important testimony. You didn't have to do that, but I did not want to put him on the stand and let you open Pandora's box about his past and his knowledge of the heroin, etc. etc. You probably could not have used it against him at trial under current law, but it spares me from having Judge Wilson knowing about it and perhaps, not being able to be uninfluenced about it in deciding the motion. I know you have been a straight shooter with me in the past on other cases, but I want to give you a little something for your kindness, no matter which way the judge rules. You know the bond is 25 grand here, so I stand to make at least $2,500. It's only right you get 2 for what you did for me.

Theos: Listen Roger, we've only been friends for a short while now and nothing along the lines you suggest is necessary. Maybe someday you can return the favor and help me out in some way. Besides, you probably should win the motion on the merits given the shoddy police work we heard about, let alone the fact his partner Andy didn't even bother to show up.

Flynn: It sure came out good for me and I've given Wilson plenty to hang his hat on. But, knowing Wilson, whether it's good on the merits does not matter. The next time he rules in my favor on the merits alone will be the first time. He knows the bond amount, and the least amount I stand to make, $2,500. Besides, he put me on the case and without his appointment, I would not have had brother Amos as a client. Based on past experience, he'll want 5 in this case. I don't want him to be disappointed. And if all goes well for me, it won't go well for you. So don't take it personally when you lose the motion. It's just the way the game is played.

One week later, in the late afternoon with only Judge Wilson, a court reporter, Peter Theos, and Roger Flynn present, Judge Wilson announces his ruling on Defendant Amos Tripp's Motion to Suppress Evidence seized on May 20, 1977. The court transcript reflects the following:

Wilson: I have carefully considered the evidence I have heard by way of testimony and documents, and here are my findings:

1. Although two Chicago Police Officers participated in Defendant Tripp's arrest and seizure from his car, only one officer testified at the hearing. With credibility of witnesses so important here, I fail to understand the absence of one of the two arresting officers, and no explanation as to his absence was ever offered.

2. The testimony of Officer George Spangler left much to be desired. The conduct supposedly giving rise to the car stop in the first instance is absent from the police report. Not only is this a glaring omission, it is incomprehensible. Additionally, if Tripp really did give consent to search—a dubious proposition at best since he knew of a kilo of heroin hidden therein—it would have been a simple matter to solidify the consent and document it accordingly. Throw into the mix Tripp's denial of consent being given, the more reasonable possibility, and it just adds to the State's difficult burden of proof. I therefore conclude that not only was there no probable cause for the stop, the search and seizure cannot stand. Even assuming a proper stop and later-developed suspicious circumstances, there was simply no valid consent given to search the car. The Motion to Suppress is, therefore, granted.

Within a few minutes after the ruling, Roger Flynn made his way back to Judge Wilson's chambers. Nobody else was present besides Judge Wilson and Defense Counsel Roger Flynn.

Flynn addressed Wilson, "Judge, I want to congratulate you on your scholarly decision. You sounded like a Supreme Court Justice in the way you analyzed the case and expressed your findings."

"I appreciate your compliment Roger, but I hope you're not saying you didn't need my help on this one," responded Wilson.

"Oh, absolutely not, Judge. I just want you to know how scholarly it was, but I know that, without you I never would have had the client. Will five do for everything?"

"Five will be fine. Thank you very much." ⚖

Peter Theos and Roger Flynn saw a good bit of each other in a number of cases in Judge Wilson's courtroom. As often as he could, Theos showed Flynn more than the usual courtesies a prosecutor might show a defense lawyer. None of these amounted to great favors, but were the kind of thing helpful to a solo criminal practitioner who might have a number of cases up in different courtrooms on the same day. The professional contacts soon gravitated to personal ones, including having drinks together after the work day.

Sharing drinks then morphed into occasional dinners between the two of them. They shared stories about their families, their likes and dislikes, and the difficulties the professional practice of law would often present. Some of what Theos said to Flynn was false and contrived, but much of it was true. As good an actor as Theos was becoming, it was simply not possible to create an identity that was fictional in most of its significant aspects. And in spite of himself, Theos gradually came to like Flynn, a man with no pretenses but, not surprisingly, dripping with charm.

Flynn liked to drink and Theos had to pretend he did too. Nothing loosens a man's tongue like alcohol, and the limits of conversations were unaffected by the intimacy of the topics covered. Bit by bit, Flynn described the problems he and his wife Peggy were having in Peggy getting and staying pregnant. The Flynns experienced a series of miscarriages, with each one adding pressure to their already strong desire to have children as a necessary part of family life.

It was during these discussions when Roger Flynn's deep love for Peggy was manifested. Roger's own humanity and concern for others gushed from his words and conduct, and Theos saw that aspect of his decency even as the extent of his legal corruption was also being unabashedly described. The adage, "hate the sin and love the sinner," was getting harder and harder to harmonize, even as Theos knew it must be for Operation Greylord to succeed.

The evidence of the closeness that was developing between Flynn and Theos arrived in the mail to Theos' home in early fall. It was an invitation from Roger and Peggy Flynn to the christening of Cynthia Flynn, a daughter born after a series of miscarriages suffered by Peggy. Cynthia was the first, and likely only, child to be carried to term by Peggy. As Roger would describe Cynthia to Peter in the frequent get-togethers they were having after Cynthia was born, Peter saw the joy that only a long hoped-for child could bring to a devoted set of parents.

Peter was, himself, nurturing the hope of having children with his girlfriend Joan, when the time was right for marriage. The unbridled happiness displayed by Roger after Cynthia was born only strengthened Peter's commitment to follow suit someday. There was no question that the Theos' would attend the christening even as Peter was imagining the consequences to the Flynns should Operation Greylord be successful and ensnare Roger Flynn. Peter knew it was best for him to not even remotely think about that possibility.

The christening was held on a beautiful fall morning at St. Carthage church on the south side of Chicago. Although St. Carthage regularly scheduled christenings for more than one child at a time, such was the stature of Roger Flynn at his church that baby Cynthia was to be the only child christened that morning. Peter and Joan arrived early and when the Flynns saw them prior to the service, they came over to greet them. Introductions of the ladies were made just after Roger embraced Peter in the most pronounced of bear hugs, accompanied by, "Peter, I am so happy you honored us by your presence. I guess it's not manly to say this, Peter, but you are becoming my closest friend."

Peter responded, "I feel the same way, Roger, and I know how much Cynthia must mean to you after all Peggy and you went through to have her. Someday, Joan and I want to experience the same happiness as you and Peggy. And when that happens, I'll want both of you there for us."

After the touching service was completed, accompanied by tears of joy from Flynn's family and good friends, the reception was held in a nearby upscale restaurant in a private room for such occasions. Including Peter and Joan, there were about 30 people in attendance for a mid-day bountiful lunch.

As Peter surveyed those in attendance he realized that he and Joan were the only couple who were neither relatives nor long term friends. Roger introduced Peter to everyone as a regular adversary of his as an Assistant State's Attorney assigned to Judge Wilson's courtroom. Roger explained that virtually all the cases were drug cases of a fairly routine nature and that Peter was an excellent lawyer whose word was his bond. Roger said that even though Peter was his adversary, he was a good friend as well and one he was proud to have. ⚖

As time passed in the fall of 1980, both the court and social contacts between Theos and Flynn increased steadily. The intimacy of their contacts also increased as it became apparent that Flynn was profiting handsomely from appointments to defendants by Judge Wilson and, in some instances, by favorable rulings he was receiving. Flynn made it plain that Judge Wilson, like some other judges hearing criminal cases, expected and received appreciation in the form of cash from the defense lawyers who were benefitting by his appointments and rulings.

Under federal law, the only way to wiretap a telephone conversation or plant a bug (a receiving and transmitting device) surreptitiously and without the knowledge of the parties being intercepted and recorded is by presenting a request to a United States District Judge showing there is probable cause to believe that a crime or crimes are being committed, that the parties to the statements sought to be intercepted are committing the crimes, and the statements or conversations to be intercepted are being made in furtherance of the crimes being engaged in. Although there are other technical requirements in those cases in which the speakers are unaware of the interceptions, the above description sets forth the basic requirements for judicial authorization to wiretap the phone conversations or plant a bug on someone's premises.

The requirements under federal law to intercept a conversation believed to be criminal in nature is considerably less stringent when one of the parties to the conversation has given his or her consent to the government to intercept and record the suspect conversations. The most common occurrence in one-party consent cases is when one of the persons who gives his consent to record the conversation is, himself or herself, a law enforcement agent or is acting in concert with a law enforcement officer or officers. No prior request or presentment to a federal judge is necessary, nor is prior authorization required by the federal judge.

Such was the state of the law governing the law enforcement officers engaged in the Operation Greylord investigation. In late 1980, it had been decided that the time was ripe for Peter Theos to leave the State's Attorney's office and to set up shop as a criminal defense lawyer. Theos arranged to meet with Flynn to tell him of his plans to leave the office and become a criminal defense lawyer. In arranging an evening meeting at a quiet bar, Theos said that he had seen how others made the same transition and had done well financially. He believed he should be able to do the same. Out of friendship, Flynn offered to help in any way he can. Theos came to the meeting wearing a wire. The later typed transcript of the meeting reads as follows:

Flynn: Hi Pete, how are you?

Theos: I'm well, Roger. And you?

Flynn: I'm doing terrific. I had a great day in a matter before Judge Lunden at a North Side Branch Court, and I feel on top of the world. Drinks are on me tonight.

Theos: Tell me what happened.

Flynn: I sure will, because I can trust you. I can't say that about a lot of guys in our business. Some of them would turn on you in a minute if it came to saving their own ass, but I think you know how I feel about you.

Theos: Rog, the feeling is mutual.

Flynn: Have you ever been before Lunden on a case?

Theos: Sad to say, I have. As a prosecutor, he screwed me royally one time and pitched a case on me. Maybe if I appear before him someday as a defense lawyer, that tiny conscience he might still have will serve to even the score with me, even though I'll be on the other side. Here's hoping, anyway. But I digress. Did he give you a kiss, today?

Flynn: He sure did; he really puckered up, today. I needed all the help I could get, and he came through like a champ.

Theos: Tell me about it.

Flynn: Here's the story. I've got a two-time loser in front of him; two DUI's in the space of the last few years and he's staring at his third one. Only this time, it's really aggravated. He's out drinking all evening, and he's ready to go home. It's almost midnight. The guys loaded to the gills, and a couple of his buddies try to stop him from driving. This asshole jumps in his car and takes off as fast as the car would go. Wouldn't you know it, a car is coming toward him and, sure enough, my guy hits him head on. The other car is being driven by a young guy who is home from college for the weekend. The kid is a terrific football player and as nice as they come, based on the evidence. He's not under the influence, but since he just pulled out himself, he's not wearing a seat-belt, hasn't had time to put it on. The collision sounded like a bomb going off, and the college kid winds up flying into the steering wheel and the windshield.

Theos: Did the kid make it?

Flynn: Yeah, he made it. But he might have been better off if he didn't. He'll never walk again, and his mind comes in and out. The doctors are hopeful that with lots of therapy, his mental faculties will come back all the way, but he's definitely never going to be the same.

Theos: Some cases are just impossible to defend. You don't have any one thing you can use other than, I suppose, the consequences to your own client's family.

Flynn: At least I had that; a great wife and two little kids. How many lives can you ruin with your stupidity, your weakness? My guy messed up his own family's future besides the college kid. Too much sadness to go around. My client deserves to go away for a long time.

Theos: So what did you do? What did you argue?

Flynn: Well, we had to plead. You can't take a case like that to trial.

Theos: Of course not.

Flynn: Not surprisingly, the ASA was coming down hard, as he should have. He wanted 10 years or more for my guy.

Theos: Did you cut a deal of any kind?

Flynn: No, I couldn't deal. I decided we would have to take our chances with Lunden. I didn't know if I could do anything with him, it was just such a heater case. But I have been before him on other cases, if you know what I mean, so I had some hope it would not come out exactly the way the prosecutor wanted.

Theos: Did your guy have any money? What were his circumstances?

Flynn: He is just a blue-collar guy, but his wife's family is in pretty good shape. They've bailed him out before, and I think they were the ones who came up with the fee. I set the fee high because of the nature of the case and, in case I could do something, to take care of all the expenses.

Theos: Did you know what the judge was going to do?

Flynn: No, I didn't have a chance to talk to him at all; too much press around, too much heat. But Lunden knows me from before, and I'm sure he had that in mind to the extent he could fade the heat.

Theos: Did the ASA come on strong with his 10 years plus?

Flynn: He was breathing fire.

Theos: How did you handle it?

Flynn: Well, like I told you, I had to emphasize the consequences to my guy's family besides the victim's family. I told Lunden that my client was just weak, not evil, and people like him can get help and become decent again. Pure punishment and a long prison sentence do not solve anything, and it costs a lot for his care and feeding over the years. I stressed the virtue of rehabilitation as the more humane approach and pleaded for everyone's understanding. I got my guy to apologize to everyone, particularly to the family, to society, to the judge, and everyone else.

Theos: How did your client perform?

Flynn: Well, he was as sincere as you would want. Thank God he was genuine about his remorse, because that came through. That gave Lunden something to rely on and justify what he was going to do.

Theos: So how did it all come out?

Flynn: Since straight probation was not in the cards—even Lunden knew that—he gave him 2 years and put him on probation for 10 years after he gets out of prison with a bunch of conditions attached, including staying off the bottle.

Theos: Not bad, not bad.

Flynn: It was as good as it could be. By putting him in jail for awhile,

Lunden muted any firestorm that no jail time would have generated. He also lectured the hell out of my client, and it made it seem the punishment was even greater than it really was. Lunden gave him a 2 year sentence and a 10 year lecture.

Theos: Is that the end of it?

Flynn: Not with Lunden, it's not. He caught my eye as we were winding up and I have seen that look before. I know what it means.

Theos: Can you even do that on a case like this with all the press it received?

Flynn: Gotta do it, but Lunden knows we have to wait and let everything die down some. He knows it will be awhile, but we both know it's going to happen.

Theos: Can I ask the range you're talking about? You see, I have come to a decision about leaving the office; I'm going to do it. I know we've talked about it before, but I finally made up my mind about it. I need to know how to deal with guys like Lunden.

Flynn: Well, congratulations. I think it's a good move for you. You have put in your time as a public servant, and now it's your chance to go out and make some money. I'll help you all I can and make available my resources as you start out. Are you hooking up with a firm?

Theos: No, I decided against that. I have made a lot of contacts while I've been here, and you have been so helpful to me. I want you to know how much I appreciate all you have done for me.

Flynn: Just so you know, you can ask me for anything. If you are going to go solo and need some temporary office space, you've got it. We'll put your name on the door. I have some space you can have, we'll get you a telephone line—the works. And there is not going to be any cost; you'll need to economize in the beginning. I'd love for you to be connected with me, because I know what a good lawyer you are, and what a good friend you have shown yourself to be.

Theos: Roger, I appreciate your generous offer of space, etc., and I may well take you up on it, at least in the beginning. Plus, you have been helpful in introducing me to people I need to know, including some judges I never appeared before, and I know your help in that regard will come in handy.

Flynn: Anything that you want that I can do, you just name it. As for your question about Lunden, he and I both know what a big favor he did for my client and his family and, although I never met him on the case, he knows I will take care of him and treat him right. That will all be taken care of in due course, and he knows and trusts me. In some ways, he's a lot like Wilson. They help you when they can, and they trust you to do the right thing. Now let me buy you a drink to celebrate your decision to go out into the real world and practice in a way they don't teach in law school.

Theos: I am eager to learn. And thank you for everything.

Soon after his meeting with Flynn, Theos left the State's Attorney's office and set up an office as a criminal defense lawyer. Around the time of the transition and while still acting undercover in the Operation Greylord investigation, Theos received a phone call from United States Attorney Brandon Hartnett. Hartnett told Theos that they would like to make Theos a Special Agent of the FBI, a job Theos always dreamed of.

After asking Theos if he would like to officially join the FBI, Theos remained speechless. Breaking the silence, Hartnett asked Theos what his answer was. Theos, near tears, told Hartnett that his dream had always been to be a Special Agent of the FBI. He tried to express to Hartnett his joy at being asked to participate in ferreting out corruption in the Cook County judicial system, even in the face of the enormous risks involved. His law license was precious to him, but he willingly joined up and accepted the risks.

Theos spoke admiringly of the FBI's work on Greylord so far, and now to be a formal part of it was all he could ask for. Theos was directed to a suburban warehouse which had been rented by the FBI and was being used to store equipment necessary to create and record phony cases to be put into state court.

As the necessity of secrecy was an ever present consideration, the only people at the induction ceremony were U.S. Attorney Hartnett, First Assistant Ben Jones, AUSA Dan Hogan and Harry Meredith, FBI Special Agent in Charge (SAC) of the Chicago office. The cast was assembled in a small, nondescript office in the warehouse building.

Hartnett greeted everyone in attendance. "Good morning, everybody. Thanks for assembling on short notice. You all know Peter Theos has wanted to be a Special Agent with the FBI for as long as he can remember. That dream is coming true this morning." Hartnett then recognized Jones.

"As I told the boss here, we got approval to do that from both the Attorney General and Director Josh Dillon. They both thought there was no better time to do this and waived all the normal application processes to get it done. It was only an hour ago that I told Peter about getting approval to do it."

Theos, still moved by the news, said, "I can't tell you how happy this makes me. But what about the four-month training period for new agents at Quantico?

Hartnett quickly responded, "That probationary period has also been waived. Greylord is going hot and heavy, and we can't afford to lose you now for that period."

Meredith then added, "The training has been waived as a condition of the position, but we plan to work it in later when we can."

Hartnett then inquired, "Has that ever been done before? Swearing in a Special Agent before he successfully completes the basic course at Quantico?

Meredith answered, "Not to my knowledge. But the time is right, we need to cover our flanks, and Peter has more than proved himself already by what he has done. So we'll make a little history this morning."

Hartnett apologized, "I'm sorry we could not invite your girlfriend, Peter. We had to keep a lid on this from everybody. You can tell her, but it has to be kept confidential, like everything else you are doing. Any other questions?"

"I'm good. Let's do it." Said Theos.

Jones asked, "Do you have the oath, Harry? You should be the one to administer the oath."

"I've got it right here. Does anyone have a camera? I'm sure Peter would like a picture."

Jones answered, "I've got one. The picture will have limited circulation."

Meredith asked, "Peter, will you please stand, raise your right hand, and repeat after me?"

"I'm ready."

With that answer, Peter Theos then repeated the oath administered by his new boss, Special Agent in Charge, Harry Meredith.

"I, Peter Theos, do solemnly swear that I will administer justice without respect to persons, and do equal right to the poor and to the rich, and that I will faithfully and impartially discharge and perform all the duties incumbent upon me as a Special Agent of the Federal Bureau of Investigation under the Constitution and laws of the United States. So help me God."

Meredith then added, "Even though swearing in a new FBI agent before he successfully completes a rigorous four month training period is a first for me and the Bureau, I thought it important to follow at least a little tradition. I brought two bottles of the most expensive champagne headquarters would approve, so let's at least celebrate in the most traditional way possible after a great event."

The bottles were opened and they popped loudly, drinks were poured all around, and congratulations and good cheer infected the celebration. After about a half hour, Hartnett said to all that it was time to get back to work. ⚖

The next step in the Greylord investigation, as daring and risky as it obviously was, would prove to be momentous. Although America is a statistics happy country, the history books do not contain an accurate record of how many times the chambers of an elected sitting judge had been infiltrated for the purpose of planting a hidden device with the capacity to intercept conversations within a defined range. The intercepted conversations were transmitted off-site and recorded for later use in criminal proceedings against the judge and possibly others. It happened in Operation Greylord.

The first step in the process required the preparation of an affidavit by a knowledgeable federal law enforcement officer setting forth an elaborate compendium of accumulated facts and circumstances to be presented to the Chief Judge of the Northern District of Illinois in order to convince the judge of the following propositions:

1. That federal criminal acts had been engaged in by the judge and/or others while in the judge's chambers;

2. That it was reasonably probable that other criminal acts and conduct would be engaged in by the judge and/or others of a similar nature in the future;

3. That the nature of the conduct, its locale, and the identity and positions of the parties make it unlikely that other and more traditional methods of investigation would disclose the evidence that would be disclosed by the electronic surveillance now being sought pursuant to Title III of the federal criminal code;

4. That no interception will be made and recorded of statements and conversations which bear no indicia of criminality by the intercepted parties;

5. That the electronic surveillance being sought will be for a limited period of time unless and until the Court grants an extension after a satisfactory application is approved for such extension.

It goes without elaboration that any such application and order granting same are secret and subject to being made public only at a later time after the issuance of a court order.

The evidentiary basis for the Title III application was the compilation of the targets' statements of the intercepted conversations and their acts of criminality that had been investigated to date. Peter Theos' knowledge and information gathered while in an undercover capacity formed a substantial part of the government's application to the judge.

It was perhaps the easy part of bugging the judge's chambers to get federal court approval. The hard part would be the effectuation of the federal judge's order: planting the bug. The questions of when, where, and how to do it were the most difficult to resolve.

An important part of the planning process was the location of the bug to be planted. That was an easy decision. Because Theos had participated in many visits to Judge Wilson's chambers, he knew the judge's habits while in chambers. Wilson invariably sat at his desk while meeting with lawyers and other visitors, irrespective of the purpose of the visits. Theos also knew that Wilson was not a regular user of drawers in his desk; that the court files were maintained by his Courtroom Deputy and not the judge.

Even though deciding to place the bug in a certain drawer in the corner of his desk was an easy call, it was a particularly sensitive one. There was not much question on anybody's part that if Judge Wilson should find the bug, the Greylord investigation would blow up and result in a premature death. The fear of an inadvertent disclosure would be a constant throughout the investigation. The belief that the ability on the part of the Greylord investigators to keep things secret and under wraps was universally held to be the single most important factor in making the progress that they had. Criminal indictments would be returned only when the investigation was as complete as possible and could go no further.

The county courthouse had excellent security in light of the large amount of public activity that took place there, including that many of its visitors were accused of crimes, often serious ones. Those who worked in and around the courthouse had identification badges. Others who did not have badges were, for the most part, regular visitors to the premises. Building maintenance men had IDs and were generally recognized by security guards. There were, however, instances of equipment failures which called for visits by non-regular workers to perform their repairs.

These features of the building required elaborate planning and preparation. It was decided that the best day to install the bug in Judge Wilson's chambers was the day after a holiday which would, itself, be celebrated by the employees and staff as part of an extended week-end. Federal holidays were often celebrated on a Monday, creating a three-day week-end. Many city, county, and state offices mimicked the federal pattern.

Most judges, including Wilson, did not come to the building on those Mondays, nor did their staff. So a certain Monday was selected. Next came the people who would do the infiltration. It was decided that two men—FBI agents—would be used. They would dress as maintenance men working for the independent contractor servicing the building. Because the Criminal Courts Building was old, equipment repairs on court holidays were not unusual. Securing appropriate personnel, uniforms, and identification cards were next on the agenda.

The maintenance men who normally serviced the building and its premises were often European natives whose conversations were characterized by accents from their home countries. The FBI scoured its available manpower to find two men with similar characteristics to plant the bug.

It was also necessary to secretly obtain or create appropriate uniforms for the agents to use. Phony IDs were prepared, as were diagrams of the building and relevant quarters. Fictional stories to cover their presence in the building should they be detained or questioned were created and rehearsed along with commitment of the building features to memory.

The Monday selected was near the end of Peter Theos' term as an Assistant State's attorney. Theos would conduct an in-depth briefing of the two undercover FBI agents as to the layout, structure, location, and elevators of the territory involved. The actual entry into the building and the path to be taken was diagrammed and studied. It was decided that Theos should not be in the area of the courtroom and chambers during the entirety of the incursion into the building and chambers, but he would have radio contact with both agents should the need arise. Everybody on the investigative team involved in the entry was sensitive to the investment of resources and unquestioned importance of the investigation. Premature disclosure would have been viewed as a disaster of the first order, especially at this point.

With every detail prepared, studied, and rehearsed, including the performances of the two "new" maintenance men, the bug was successfully planted. It would never be prematurely discovered. ⚖

Whatever else Roger Flynn may have been, he was a man of his word and loyal to his friends. In keeping with his promise to Peter Theos to help him get started in the private practice of law, Flynn went to the chambers of Judge Sam Wilson early one morning prior to Wilson taking the bench to hear his morning call. As was his custom, Flynn sauntered into Wilson's chambers after his secretary told Flynn the judge was in.

He greeted Wilson, "Hey Judge, how you doing? Hope I'm not interrupting anything."

"Nope, just taking a quick cigarette break before the next hearing. You got something up today?" asked Wilson.

"Nah. I just thought I'd come in and tell you the news if you haven't heard it already."

"What's the news?"

"Peter Theos is leaving the State's Attorney's office and going out on his own. He is going to be one of us."

Wilson, looking astonished, said, "You're kidding? How is he capable of switching sides?"

"Don't underestimate him. He's got a lot of moxie."
Wilson responded, "I'll tell you what he's got, he's got a holier than thou attitude. Righteous little bastard."

"What do you mean?"

"He always acted as if I didn't know shit about the law. He could never understand that locking everybody up for drugs was not the only solution for solving the drug problem."

Defensively, Flynn responded, "Well judge, when these guys get out of law school, they're all full of idealism. They see everything in black-and-white terms, you know, good versus evil. When they get to be prosecutors, they wrap the flag around themselves and only they know what's good for society. They're going to straighten out the world, even though it's been crooked as long as anyone can remember."

Agreeing, Wilson said, "Especially him. He's been getting fed the same philosophy all his life from his immigrant parents—put enough bad guys in jail and the world will be a safer place."

"Judge, you're being a little hard on him. He's not the saint you might think he is."

"I'll bet that's true. If you gave that little prick some truth serum, you might find that he probably dabbled a little himself. Certainly with marijuana—still an illegal substance, you know—and maybe even with that white powder stuff. A lot of those do-gooders are like that—law and order is for the other guy and not for them."

Flynn, somewhat alarmed at Wilson's vehemence, said, "Judge, Judge, Peter's not like that. I've been with him a lot, and he's not really like that. Peter is just a strong advocate, he hates to lose. Now that he is on the other side, he will fight just as hard to keep people out of jail as he once did to put them there."

"Well, let's hope so. Every time we put someone away, if their family wasn't a real mess before they got caught, it sure will be when daddy goes away. With mom working, grandma too old to help, nobody is left to control the kids. Sometimes what we do makes matters worse instead of better."

"Judge, I'm not here to disagree with you, but there are lots of other sides to your argument and I don't want us to get sidetracked. I'm just here to let you know about Peter, and to tell you I'm helping him getting started any way I can. I'm giving him some of my space to use, and am referring business to him I can't personally handle or where I have conflicts."

"I'm not surprised, Roger, because that's the kind of guy you are. I'm just not as sure as you about your friend."

"Judge, he told me that he enjoyed practicing in your court, and I believe he was very sincere in his feelings about you. Trust me, he is OK, and he knows how to play the game. Of course, it's your call, but I know he would be very appreciative if you could throw something his way if you get the chance. All I ask is for you to think about it."

"Roger, out of respect for our friendship, I'll see what I can do for Peter. Maybe he's not a bad kid, but I have to make sure I can trust him before I do trust him."

Flynn responded, "For what it's worth, I look at him like a little brother. But you're right, in the business we're in, you have to be sure you know who your friends are."

"Good to see you, Roger. Best of luck with your new roommate." The following morning, Roger Flynn and Peter Theos met at Flynn's office. Theos was wearing a wire. A transcript was prepared of the meeting, and this is how it read:

Flynn: Hey, Peter, how's it going?

Theos: Not bad, Roger. But starting your own office is a real eye opener. Practicing law seems to be the least of it. Putting business systems in place, hiring help, opening accounts, attending legal and social functions to get your name out, and just plain hustling business are not only new to me, my survival depends on it.

Flynn: You have to admit there is a real luxury when you work in an office and all that stuff is handled for you. But it will come, slowly at first, but you have to hang in and not get disillusioned.

Theos: How did you do it? Did you ever despair over whether you would make it?

Flynn: Peter, despair was my middle name. I notice you didn't mention running to banks and borrowing more money you never expected to need just to open the office doors. No matter how successful you might have been working for someone else, the bankers treat you as if you're two months away from bankruptcy. One of the questions the bank asked was my expected income for the first year. If you could be prosecuted for basing an answer on hope rather than a reasonable expectation founded on reality, I was a sitting duck for an indictment. But with the help of a few friends in our profession, and especially the kindness of certain members of our judicial brethren, I made it.

Theos: So are you saying that the despair got drowned out by the ringing of the cash register?

Flynn: Let's put it this way, dame fortune smiled my way. Some of the early years' successes have been based on luck, but when it came my way, I knew enough how to keep it going. And that is what I want to explain to you this morning. What to do when luck finds you, and how to keep it going.

Theos: I think I know where you're going with this.

Flynn: Peter, I know you well enough now to trust you. I have done so in the past, and you haven't betrayed me. I'm not going to beat around the bush in telling you how some things work in our business; I'm going to give it to you straight.

Theos: You can trust me. I'm all ears.

Flynn: There are some judges handling criminal cases in the Circuit Court of Cook County that you just have to pay in order for your client to get a fair shake or, depending on the circumstances, a little better than a fair shake.

Theos: You mean flat-out bribery?

Flynn: In some cases, yes. In other cases, you have to know the rules of the game before that particular judge. There can be some complexity and indirection in the relationship, and you absolutely must know who you are dealing with.

Theos: Are you talking system-wide?

Flynn: No, I do not handle many civil cases, so I cannot speak intelligently about judges handling civil cases. My experience is on the criminal side.

Theos: Are you saying all the judges handling criminal cases are dirty?

Flynn: Absolutely not. Many are honest. But you have to know who is who. If you make an approach to an honest judge, you will be in a world of trouble. I'm talking criminal investigation, possible prosecution, and loss of your license.

Theos: That I understand perfectly. What about the others?

Flynn: You have to know who they are, no matter your own intentions. It could be perilous for your client if you don't know whether the judge before you is playing a bad game or not.

Theos: Why is that?

Flynn: Simple. If you are before a crooked judge and you are comporting yourself honestly in that courtroom, a dishonest judge will have outcomes in cases often favoring criminal defendants. The statistics of that judge will start to look lopsided. To make things look more neutral and even-handed, the crooked judge may start favoring the prosecution in cases in which that judge does not have a special interest in that case. An honest lawyer who just wants a fair result based on the facts of the case may be subjecting his client to a harsher outcome than is called for to make up for the cases the judge goes the other way because he got paid off.

Theos: What do you do in that circumstance?

Flynn: My experience is that if an honest lawyer who does nothing improper has a case assigned to such a judge, he tells the client he will not handle the case and refuses to file an appearance for that client.

Theos: So where does that leave his now defenseless client?

Flynn: That's a very good question. In the end, the client will have to get a new lawyer. The tricky part is what the honest lawyer tells the client as to why he can no longer represent that client. A lawyer who appears before a judge he believes to be dishonest best not go around telling people about his suspicions. The consequences of making such statements are many and severe. Not having ever been in such a situation, I cannot tell you what I would do should I be faced with it. There may be no good way to handle it.

Theos: So how do you handle the, perhaps, not-so-honest judge?

Flynn: The first thing you must do is to be sure you know the character of the judge you're in front of. If you determine he is not honest, you have to decide whether, based on ethical and legal considerations, you intend to employ any means available to be successful in the defense of your client. Of course, one of the first considerations is how you got the client in the first place.

Theos: I think I know what you mean, but please be specific.

Flynn: I was going to get to that. Here's how that works, especially in Judge Wilson's courtroom. You know well the kinds of cases he hears; the preliminary stages of usually low level drug cases. These drug defendants appear before him as their first appearance, usually without a lawyer. To maintain their freedom, they usually have to post 10% of the bond amount the judge sets. The bonds usually run from $1,000 to $10,000, with the defendant posting cash between $100 and $1,000. Defendants often sign over the receipts for the bond amounts posted to their lawyers in payment of the lawyer's fee.

Theos: So what's the catch?

Flynn: The catch is this. If the judge in the courtroom likes you, he may appoint you to represent the unrepresented defendant. At this point, there is nothing illegal about the judge's appointment, since the client agrees to retain the lawyer, even though there may be representatives of bar associations present in the courtroom ready and willing to be appointed and, if the client is indigent, to not charge a fee.

Theos: So far so good. But can the appointed lawyer make money this way? I mean, maybe the CBR's are mostly $100.

Flynn: Yes, the appointed lawyer can make lots of money. Here's how: the cases don't take long before the judge; they're quite routine. It is a high- volume courtroom, so if the appointed lawyer is well liked by the judge, he will be appointed to lots of cases that day. How many CBRs does it take to generate thousands of dollars in a day? See what I mean?

Theos: I see quite well. So the catch must be how well the judge likes you, and how many cases he appoints you to.

Flynn: I see you've paid attention to your surroundings while working in Judge Wilson's court. You should now be able to figure out why the judge likes some lawyers more than others, since affection only goes so far in our profession as between judges and able lawyers.

Theos: I take it when you thank the judge for his appointments in a material way, you've left the realm of affection and entered the world of corruption.

Flynn: Right on. It may not seem that way, because the judge may only receive a small percentage of what the lawyer gets, but it adds up, just like the cash bond refunds add up. And if the judge keeps appointing you because of the gratuities you treat him to, you are, in effect, bribing him to act in that way since part of his duties are the lawyer appointment process.

Theos: It seems so small and innocent.

Flynn: Yes, it can seem that way. But it can get big and, under the strict definition of the law, it can be considered bribery. But let me tell you the more invidious feature of the practice.

Theos: Please do.

Flynn: Here's what it is. Do you think that when a judge appoints a particular lawyer to represent a criminal defendant who is appearing before him, with knowledge that a gratuity will be given for the appointment, that judge will be fair and impartial in every other decision he may have to make at a later point in the proceedings? Suppose the lawyer files a motion to suppress some evidence in the case. You were a prosecutor once. Do you think, under these circumstances, the Assistant State's Attorney is going to get a fair ruling? Now you be the judge, Mr. Theos.

Theos: It's starting to get murky.

Flynn: Just remember what side you are on now. In addition, always be sure you know your judge, including his track record and his practices.

Theos: Anything else?

Flynn: Yes. Do not ever tell a client that you are friends with a judge or that you have some relationship with him. And if you do establish some relationship with him, remember that what you do in the beginning will establish a pattern as to what is expected later. Always be reasonable, and always be polite.

Theos: I think I understand.

Flynn: You should know that I told Judge Wilson about your new practice and our friendship. I am optimistic that he will try to help you in the appointment process in his courtroom. Let me know if I can help in other ways.

Theos: Thank you for everything, Roger. ⚖

Up to this point in Operation Greylord, the necessity of secrecy had been scrupulously maintained. So long as information was developed and shared as needed within the FBI and the Department of Justice, control over its spread remained within the power of supervisors and other employees of those law enforcement agencies. The creation of fabricated cases in order to put before suspected corrupt judges as an investigative tool, however, added a different, and more difficult dimension of maintaining operational secrecy.

To minimize risk of disclosure, as well as to be as efficient as possible to get the cases before suspect judges, it became obvious that those local officials with powers of assignment and supervision would have to be informed about Operation Greylord and trusted with that knowledge. Without some assistance within the Circuit Court of Cook County and the States Attorney's Office, targeting suspect judges would be like flying blind.

In solving these problems, it was decided that the reputations of state officials did indeed matter. The Presiding Judge of the Criminal Court at 26th and California, the principal forum for criminal cases in Cook County, had a long and illustrious career as an attorney and as a judge. Not only was he known for his extraordinary abilities, he was known for his rock hard honesty and integrity. No single rumor of dishonesty had ever been heard about him. Putting trust in him was an easy decision.

The assistance of the State's Attorney was also determined to be necessary for reasons of case assignments and treatment. Because of a state election in which a new State's Attorney was elected to replace the incumbent from the opposite political party, it was necessary to consider entrusting Operation Greylord information to two people instead of just one.

Once again Dame Fortune smiled on Operation Greylord. It so happened that both occupants of the Office of State's Attorney, were unblemished in their reputations for honesty and trustworthiness.

After careful consideration by all of the federal supervisors running Operation Greylord as to the wisdom and necessity of informing those three persons of the existence of the investigation and requesting their assistance as needed, it was unanimously decided it should be done.

All three officials were approached, at various times, and solicited for their cooperation. Each person willingly signed on to the project. When history recorded the conclusion of Operation Greylord and its indisputable success, the faith and trust placed in that judge and the two prosecutors were hailed by their federal counterparts. ⚖

The following event represents a staged confrontation between two undercover FBI agents, one male and the second a female. The two are ostensibly boyfriend and girlfriend who live together, and the apartment they share has been rented by the FBI solely for this purpose. The fake scene in which only the two are present in the apartment is apparently a fight between the two of them. A loud verbal argument takes place which can be heard by other tenants in the building. The verbal argument escalates to the point, at least to the outsiders, in which a physical assault occurs. The woman appears to have suffered bruises to her face and neck. In reality, make-up is carefully applied to make it look that she has been struck and injured by her boyfriend, with fake blood added to the mix. The police are called, and the purpose of the staging is to have the undercover male agent arrested and brought before a judge in order to test the judge's honesty; the neighbors who called the police are unaware of the ruse. The neighbors are an elderly couple who have been married almost 50 years, and who are quite affected by the apparent violence engaged in by the male boyfriend. Two police officers arrive, and the elderly neighbors excitedly tell the officers what they heard coming from the apartment and what the woman looked like when she burst out of the apartment, banged on the door of the elderly couple, and asked them to call the police.

The following conversation ensued between the elderly couple and the two police officers.

"Are you the people who called the police?" asked the first officer.

The wife responded, "Yes, we are. You must hurry and help her. He threatened to kill her, and she looks so awful."

The second officer jumped in, "Did you see him hit her? Did she hit him? Tell us what you saw and heard."

"We didn't see them actually fighting. Their door was closed the whole time. But we heard him screaming at her and heard banging from inside. She kept hollering, "Don't hurt me! Don't hurt me!" and just kept on screaming. He called her a bunch of names and kept shouting at her,

"Don't do that again! Don't ever do that again!" said the husband.

The wife added, "We don't know what he meant, and she said she wouldn't do it again, but he seemed to keep hitting her like he was in a rage or something."

"What did you actually see?" the first officer asked.

"When she came to our door and asked us to call the police, she looked just awful. Beat up, bleeding, bruised. I don't understand how a man can do that to someone he's supposed to love," the wife related close to tears herself.

The second officer asked, "Are you both willing to sign statements for us in case the girlfriend refuses to press charges?"

The husband replied without hesitation, "Of course we will; just let us know."

The two officers then went next door and arrested the man in the apartment. The following conversation then took place between the undercover male and female agents and the two officers.

The first officer, turning to the woman said, "Tell us what happened. Did he hit you? What's going on?"

"Oh, we just had a disagreement about something, and my fiancée got a little out of control."

"How many times did he hit you? Where did he hit you?"

"A couple of times in the face and neck. But I think he's sorry now."

"Did you ever hit him?" "Nah, I didn't hit him at all. I admit I called him a few names, but it was nothing he hasn't heard before."

Now the second officer addressed the man, "What do you have to say for yourself?"

The male agent responded in character, "I ain't got nothing to say, just that she started it and I finished it."

"What, are you proud of yourself, you smartass?"

"Look, I know my rights and I'm not saying anything until I get a lawyer."

"You know your rights, huh? This must not be your first go round, I guess."

"I told you I have nothing to say, so do what you have to do."

"We're going to do exactly that, smart mouth. You're under arrest. Put your hands behind your back, and don't try anything cute. I'm not in love with you like your fiancée here, and am not about to take your shit."

The male agent did not resist and did as he was told. The two officers walked him to their squad car and placed him in the back seat. The two officers rode in front. En route to the station, the following conversation took place. The first officer was driving, and the second officer turned and addressed the undercover agent.

"You sure must think you're a tough guy, smacking your fiancee around like that."

"She started it and got what she had coming."

"No matter what she said to you, she didn't have that coming to her, Mr. Tough Guy."

"You weren't there, so you don't know what she said or did."

"No, I wasn't there then, but I'm here now."

The second officer then turned to his partner, "Stop the car at the next alley. I want to see how tough this guy is when he's facing someone his own size."

The first officer pulled into an alley and stopped the car. The second officer directed the agent to get out of the car; the agent did so, although his hands were cuffed in front of his body at that point.

As the agent struggled to get out of the car and stand beside it, the second officer approached him and delivered two rapid punches to the agent's stomach. He said to the agent, "You ain't so tough now big boy. Now get back in the car before I decide to take the cuffs off and really test what you're made of. And don't bother crying to somebody that I hit you twice. There's no marks to back up your story and you beating up a girl like you did stamps you a coward. Nobody will believe you."

Whereupon, the two officers drove to the police station and booked the agent without further incident. ⚖

Not every concocted incident devised for Operation Greylord was going to be executed according to plan. Murphy's Law—if something can go wrong, it will—did not have an exception for law enforcement agents intent on cleansing the local courts of judicially related corruption. This is what happened next.

A plan was drafted in which two undercover FBI agents would appear to be slightly under the influence of alcohol. The site selected as the venue was a popular bar on the near north side of Chicago. One of the two undercover agents was about 6'4" tall, well-built and weighed 240 lbs. The other undercover agent was smaller, about 5'10" tall and about 180 lbs.

The plan was for them to engage in an argument in the bar, become much louder and hostile, and be arrested. It was expected that the arrested agent would be detained that evening, but he would be brought before a judge the following morning for the necessary judicial proceedings. Bond was expected to be set by the judge in a normal amount with other undercover agents ready to post it with official funds secured for the purpose.

Shortly after midnight, the two agents, while in the bar and appearing slightly intoxicated, began a loud argument over the feminine virtues of a mutual acquaintance. The argument escalated and was laced with profanity; their actions were disruptive of business. After both were escorted out of the bar by the bouncers, each of the combatants challenged the masculinity and toughness of the other.

The larger agent appeared to land a punch to the head of the smaller agent, and the vial of fake blood became evidence of the fierceness of the dispute. Three other undercover agents appeared to act as peacemakers, but one of the bouncers called the police at the first sight of the fake blood.

In short order, the police arrived. Seeing the smaller of the two combatants bleeding profusely, the agent who threw the punch was pointed out by some bystander witnesses. He was immediately arrested and taken into custody by the police.

As expected, the arrested agent was processed by the police at about 1 a.m., but remained in custody until 10 a.m. the next morning to set bond. No undercover FBI lawyer was available to represent the agent, so an Assistant Public Defender was summoned for the bond hearing. As part of his preparation, the Assistant State's Attorney interviewed the two arresting police officers before the end of their shift. The two police officers gave the ASA an earful about the disparity in size between the man arrested who punched and pummeled the smaller man. Because of the profusion of blood, the police officers believed that the smaller man suffered serious injuries.

The ASA, being recently hired as a prosecutor, was moved by the account of the incident from the two officers. The ASA was determined for a high bond to be set because of the force used by a big man on a smaller man, and the belief that serious injury was the result. The Assistant Public Defender, unaware of the true state of affairs about the incident and having very little to argue by way of mitigation and no sympathy for his client's position, was less than impassioned in his resistance to a high bond. His argument for the release of his client was perfunctory, while the prosecutor's argument was impassioned and vigorous.

The hearing judge, reflecting the disparity in the presentations of the lawyers, set bond in the amount of $100,000. To be released would require the arrested agent to post 10% of the amount set, or $10,000. The other undercover agents did not have that sum to post, resulting in the undercover agent being remanded to the custody of the state.

As a consequence of the bond setting, the arrested agent remained in jail the rest of that day and the following night. That evening, as the inmates were lining up for the evening meal, an inmate sidled up to the agent. The inmate was accompanied by two other inmates, all three of whom bore similar tattoos that the agent recognized as that of a prominent street gang in Chicago with a reputation for drug dealing and violence. The first inmate, referred to by his two cohorts as "Heavy," appeared to be a least 6'5" tall and at least 280 lbs. All three of the men looked physically fit, and "Heavy" looked beyond fit; imposing would have been a more apt description. The following dialogue took place:

Heavy, leaning close to the agent's face, said, "Hey man, what's up?"

The undercover agent, backing up, replied, "Not too much."

"The word going around is that you're pretty good with your fists."

"I don't know about all that, but I take care of myself when I have to."

"Hey, man, I've never seen you here before, so I don't know if you're up to what goes on around here."

"What do you mean?"

Heavy explained. "Well, it sometimes gets boring with not much to do so some of the guards arrange a little time and space for us to sort of test each other out. You know, let us do our own version of the Friday night fights. We set up a ring out in the yard, one of the guards is the referee, another is the timer. You know, just like the pros."

"You mean with gloves and all?"

"Yeah, man. The whole nine yards. Betting and all. It breaks the monotony.

"I'm impressed."

"You impressed enough to take me on? I'm the champ now, and your arrest and what you did to that guy got here ahead of you. I'm getting rusty, 'cause nobody wants to take me on. You game?"

"I'm game enough, but I'm looking to get out of here."

Heavy, exasperated, replied, "Look man, we're all looking to get out of here, but we're all on the inside right now. What do you say? We can set it up for tomorrow night. Our Friday night fights, right here in Cook County Illinois. Except no TV, but all the rest."

"Let's put it this way; if I'm here tomorrow night, you're on."

"Good deal. I told my boys you ain't a coward."

The panic did not take long to set in. The first order of business was to get word to the FBI about the urgency of the situation. A call to the incarcerated defendant's "lawyer" had to be arranged.

After request for access to a phone, the agent took his place in a line that one sees when free merchandise is handed out. It was longer than the length of a football field. When the call was finally made, the answering FBI agent lawyer gulped noticeably when told he had to secure $10,000 in cash as quickly as possible. The red tape to do so was too complicated to describe. Additionally, posting this large amount had its own urgency. The Court Clerk's officers who approve bond deposits do not resemble 24-hour ATM machines in their hours of operation. Through the entire process of waiting, the incarcerated agent thought he better start thinking about boxing strategies and began shadow boxing in preparation. In the nick of time, the $10,000 was posted and the incarcerated agent left the jail in a record sprint. Only Heavy was the disappointed one. ⚖

In what may be the busiest court in the United States, the Traffic Court was commissioned to handle all of the traffic violations occurring in Cook County, Illinois. Hundreds of thousands of cases went through the system on an annual basis. The range of offenses ran from violations for running stop signs to speeding to driving while intoxicated.

There was hardly an adult citizen with a driver's license living in the county who never, at some point or other, had to appear there in defense of an alleged traffic violation. The citizens' view of the criminal justice system often began and ended with their experiences in Traffic Court.

For those charged with minor violations, justice was meted out with a conveyor belt quality. Some defendants beat the charges and saved themselves the cost of a fine, albeit inconvenienced by the necessity of taking time to appear in court and, on occasion, the cost of a lawyer. For those charged with more serious violations—those facing stiff fines and possible incarceration if found guilty—the experiences were quite different. The fear of conviction and possible jail time was enough to make the experience a lasting memory. Even an acquittal would mean a substantial financial undertaking because of the need to hire a lawyer.

Self-representation might be OK and not foolhardy for the minor charges, but invariably foolish if invoked by defendants faced with serious consequences should they be found guilty. These circumstances dictated the need for attorney representation as well as driving the cost for the services of counsel.

Because of its size and importance, Traffic Court had its own presiding judge. Although located in a single building in downtown Chicago, there were a number of courtrooms in the building. Some of the judges assigned to Traffic Court were permanently assigned there, while other judges would regularly rotate in and out for designated periods of time.

Although most of the courtrooms were similar in size and layout, the employees in the building and the regular practitioners there referred to the courtrooms either as a "big room" or a "small room."

Those designations were based on the types of violations heard in each. The more serious cases were heard in the big rooms and the minor cases were heard in the small rooms.

The courtroom designations also dictated which assigned judges sat in which courtrooms. Permanently assigned judges to Traffic Court usually sat in the big rooms and temporarily assigned judges sat in the small rooms.

As was well known, only one political party held the major offices in the county for as long as anyone could remember. Because the volume of business conducted in Traffic Court was so substantial, it was necessary to employ dozens and dozens of staff people at the building. The patronage system was in full bloom there. Courtroom deputies, court clerks, secretaries, police officers, maintenance help and others made up the cadre of personnel in the work force besides the judges and their law clerks.

Then, of course, there were the lawyers. Members of the State's Attorney's office prosecuted many of the cases, along with lawyers from the Chicago Corporation Counsel's office. On the defense side were attorneys from the Public Defender's office, counsel from the Chicago Bar Association and, of course, private counsel.

The make-up of private counsel was two-fold. The first group consisted of lawyers who did not regularly practice in Traffic Court, but appeared selectively on a retained basis. The other group consisted of private lawyers who were always present in Traffic Court and appeared to specialize in and handle only cases in the Traffic Court building. This latter group was not large in number, but always seemed to have a steady stream of clients. More often than not, they seemed to represent most of the defendants who had cases in the big rooms.

Emancipated from his obligations as an Assistant State's Attorney and the strictures imposed by the office, Peter Theos' life became a whirlwind of activity. Even though ostensibly pursuing private practice for greater professional and financial success, Theos' priority was the advancement of Operation Greylord. Although not privy to everything the United States Attorney's office was doing in that regard, he was sufficiently trusted to be told of events he was not personally involved in.

There were compelling reasons for that level of trust. By virtue of his employment as an ASA, Theos had the closest connection to the States Attorney's office and the scuttlebutt which always exists in offices of that kind. He knew many of the players in that office, including the group of public defenders regularly defending cases the prosecutors brought. Theos also was acquainted with the private defense bar regularly handling state criminal cases. He had seen several of the goings on in the criminal courtrooms and heard about even more. He also had first-hand experience in Traffic Court. In addition to having personal knowledge about people and events, he developed well thought-out suspicions about what was taking place.

Many outcomes of cases had reasonable explanations. Because of limited resources with which to work, these matters could be ignored. In other cases and outcomes, results defied reason, logic, and experience. When coupled with bits and pieces of information Theos picked up due to his position, his suspicions were often well grounded. For these reasons as well as his demonstrated abilities as a lawyer, Theos was not only a valuable resource to the federal government in Operation Greylord, he was a unique contributor in the direction the investigation took.

For example, a great source of knowledge as to whether matters were being handled and resolved properly by judges was information shared by prosecutors themselves. The bulk of the trials conducted in the big rooms of Traffic Court, the more serious cases, were prosecuted by permanently assigned assistants. Theos knew that a disproportionate number of these defendants were represented by a handful of defense lawyers—perhaps numbering from six to eight or so—who seemed to be in the building each day from morning to night.

What was unusual about these lawyers, in addition to their constant presence in the Traffic Court buildings, was their extraordinary success in the outcomes of their cases. Many of the cases were bench trials, in which the presiding judge was the fact finder as opposed to a jury of randomly selected citizens. In other matters, whether in hearings, rulings, or sentences imposed when a defendant may have been found guilty, the judges' decisions generally had a defendant's slant as opposed to the prosecution.

Indeed, the overall success rate of this handful of ever-present lawyers was, if statistically and randomly analyzed, neither reasonable nor understandable. When the evidence was objectively assessed in many of the cases, the outcomes were unjustifiable.

The assigned prosecutors to Traffic Court regularly shared their displeasures with each other and with other prosecutors in other divisions of their office. Indeed, the select group of highly successful defense lawyers came to be known over time as miracle workers.

Adding to the anomylous nature of the results in favor of the miracle workers was the contrary trend of the results in cases represented by the public defenders. As is common in America, indigent defendants in felony criminal cases are entitled to legal representation provided by a unit of government. The public defenders assigned to Traffic Court were as experienced and skilled as the miracle workers, and the nature of the cases handled by public defenders were similar to those handled by the miracle workers in all material respects, including the quality of evidence presented at trial.

A comparison of a sample size of outcomes between the two groups of lawyers in major cases defied comprehension and explanation. Not only was this differential obvious, but it was a constant source of complaint and angst among the public defenders. Their complaints about constantly losing their cases while the miracle workers were constantly winning theirs led to frequent complaints and suspicions, mostly voiced within their own group.

Nevertheless, Theos' antenna was now finely refined and far-reaching.

Other imponderables were the constant presence of the miracle workers and their open and obvious solicitations of clients in the Traffic Court building. They roamed the hallways at-will and conducted their business in the washrooms and other public areas of the buildings. The rules of ethics governing the conduct of lawyers clearly prohibited the solicitation of business by lawyers. The miracle workers operated in an almost brazen fashion in their trolling of the public for clients, and were never seen to be stopped by any of the judges assigned to Traffic Court or the Presiding Judge of the Court.

Other evidence of favoritism included the easy familiarity the miracle workers enjoyed with court clerks and other court staff. While it is not improper to be shown some courtesies, it is of great benefit to courtroom lawyers to have their cases called promptly and not have to wait in a queue. For lawyers, time is money.

Specific instances of odd and unexplainable conduct also came to Theos' attention. On one occasion, a particularly disgruntled prosecutor angrily described an incident in which he was prosecuting a young woman for driving while intoxicated. On direct examination, the defendant testified to having had a couple of beers just before leaving a gathering at a bar. On cross-examination, the prosecutor got the defendant to admit she may have had more than a couple of beers. When the prosecutor asked her if she in fact could feel the effect of the beers, she answered yes. At that point, one of the miracle workers asked for an immediate recess, which the judge granted.

After the break, the young woman resumed the stand and, upon redirect examination by her miracle worker lawyer, recanted her answer that she felt the beers and said she was simply mistaken on cross. Shortly thereafter, the defendant rested her case. The brief argument to the judge by the prosecutor, in addition to the bystanders' testimony that the defendant was impaired at the time of the event, emphasized her own admission on the stand to the same effect. The miracle worker argued, with a straight face, that the defendant was simply mistaken in her testimony while ignoring the testimony of the bystanders. The whole of the judge's ruling was, "I still have a reasonable doubt. I find her not guilty."

Peter Theos included all the above information, as well as other inexplicable conduct occurring at Traffic Court, to his superiors in Operation Greylord. Included in his discussion was a delineation of all of the judges and court employees about whom he had suspicions as to their honesty and the reasons and information in support of his views.

A later meeting between Peter Theos and the Operation Greylord supervisory personnel resulted in the targeting of subjects and the methods to be followed in furthering the investigation. Although there were many honest judges and employees working at the Traffic Court during the relevant period of the investigation, the prosecutive results reflected that it was the site of a cesspool of corruption so deep that it had become institutionalized.

Among other things, rumors were strong that the miracle workers' ability to solicit clients at Traffic Court and, in effect, use the building as their offices, was due to the close relationship they had with the Presiding Judge of the Court. The belief among the many honest lawyers regularly assigned to the courthouse was that the freedom to do so by the miracle workers was bought and paid for. The other belief indulged was that the outcomes of cases which were contrary to reasonable assessments of the evidence were also bought and paid for, with the assigned judges being the main suspects.

The Operation Greylord investigation therefore targeted the miracle workers, the judges issuing hard-to-understand verdicts, and various court personnel assigned to or associated with those judges.

When Operation Greylord finally ended and the prosecutions were completed, the final results demonstrated conclusively the truth of those beliefs. ⚖

Judge Henry Largo was a veteran in the Circuit Court of Cook County. After initially serving as a general trial judge in the system, he was given a number of supervisory positions. The most recent promotion had been from Presiding Judge of Traffic Court to Presiding Judge of the First Municipal District. In his new role, many courts were under his supervision, including Traffic Court and all the branch courts in the district.

Judge Stanley Casper was assigned to Branch Court 29, which was in the First Municipal District. Casper was known as a maverick political figure, perhaps owing to the fact that the Cook County Democratic Central Committee had never recommended him for the judgeship he held. Casper, a naturalized Polish-American citizen, was popular with the voters, however.

As a practicing lawyer in his community, his reputation for honesty, knowledge of the law, hard work, and devotion to his clients was sterling. Casper's fees were reasonable, given the blue collar nature of the clients who flocked to his office. He was also admired for "forgetting" to always charge those clients who could not afford to pay even his normal charges. Sensitive to their need for his services, but mindful of the dignity of their character, he would insist that they pay modest amounts whenever they could afford it. In that way, the term "freeloader" could not be applied to any of them.

Casper's social conscience and the kindnesses he provided to his community were repaid many times over at the ballot box. In his one and only contested election, and notwithstanding the Democratic Party's endorsement of his opponent and its all-out support to the endorsed candidate during the election, Casper garnered 90% of the vote. In two subsequent elections, Casper ran unopposed.

Once he was elected, Casper's reputation for honesty and integrity on the bench was quickly established. He also became known as a no nonsense jurist with little tolerance for the procrastinators and the unprepared. In spite of his high ratings by the bar associations, Casper did not often get the plum assignments by his supervisors. Undaunted, Casper was determined to be the best judge he could possibly be, loyal to the maxim that virtue is its own reward.

Having finished his call early one day, and never having met Judge Largo, Casper thought it would be a nice touch to go downtown and introduce himself to his new boss and get acquainted with him. Not wanting to just barge in on him and wanting assurance that Judge Largo could meet with him in chambers, Casper asked his secretary to arrange a brief visit for the afternoon. She did so and informed Casper that Judge Largo would be pleased to meet with him.

A quick ride on the CTA brought Judge Casper to the Daley Center, and he was soon in Judge Largo's reception area. After being ushered into the Presiding Judge's chambers, Casper greeted Judge Largo. "Good morning, Henry. Since we have never met, I wanted to come down to see you and to congratulate you on your appointment."

"Good afternoon, Stanley. I think we have never met, even though we have both been at this judging business for a few years now. It is awfully nice on your part to take the time to come downtown and wish me well in my new assignment. It is so thoughtful on your part."

"Well, I finished my call early and had the time to get downtown, "replied Casper.

"I must admit I am not as familiar with the branch courts as I should be, having spent my career down here. The last years I have been presiding at Traffic Court, and you probably know how busy that court is on a daily basis. It is hard to get out of that building, even to grab a quick bite," replied Largo.

"I know that's true, Henry, and that is one of the benefits of branch court. Although we're busy every day, it sure isn't like what you guys have to deal with in Traffic."

"Even though I'm new to the job involving the whole municipal district, I have reviewed a bunch of reports and statistics about the branch courts, including yours. I can tell from the numbers that all of you at Branch 29 are really turning out the cases and things seem to be running smoothly. Am I right about that?" asked Largo. "Tell me if there is anything I can do to help you out there and make things a little easier for you."

Casper responded, "Well, I appreciate your offer. There is one thing that you might be able to help with, and that is this. I know you're familiar with the workings in Traffic Court where a lot of lawyers—regular practitioners there—hang around the hallways and solicit business from those people who don't have their own lawyers. We have a lot of those guys in the branch courts, and they're hard to keep out. They just ignore any signs we put up saying soliciting clients is both unethical and against the rules of our court, and don't pay any attention to us when we tell them they can't do that and chase them away.

These guys leave when we tell them that, but they're back in five minutes and carrying on as if we never had that conversation."

"What do you suggest I do?" asked Largo.

"Well, here's what I did and it works in my court. The way these guys get paid is to have their clients sign over the Cash Bond Refunds. Of course, the judges have to approve the assignment, so in my courtroom, I just refused to approve the assignment to those lawyers. The lawyers then have to chase their clients for their fees, and you can guess how successful they are. The case is over, the client received his services, and the lawyer doesn't have any leverage over his now discharged client. The lawyers bitch to me that they should not be in the collection agency business, but I tell them they should not be soliciting legal business in the hallways and the washrooms in the first place. The word is out that I will refuse to approve the assignments to these regulars, and so they no longer appear in my courtroom. It works like a charm."

"So how can I help?" asked Largo. "It seems you have already come up with a solution."

"It works great for me, so I thought that if you issued some directive or order to all of the judges in the branch courts never approve these

CBRs that are assigned to these guys, their work will dry up and they'll have to start acting ethically in their pursuit of business."

"Are you proposing that we ban any assignment of a CBR to a lawyer, even if that lawyer is not one of the regulars at that branch court? Aren't assignments legal? Can we stop a legal practice to get at the underlying unethical practice of overt solicitation?" asked Largo.

Casper said, "Why not? It works in my courtroom. Besides, it is only a rare case where the assignment of the CBR to the lawyer was not one of these regular hustlers. If we did it system wide, we could get rid of these shady practices and restore some dignity to our handling of cases and bring improvement to our profession. I'm telling you Henry, it will work. If you cut off the money stream, that will end this hustling business."

After a prolonged silence, Largo said, "I'm going to have to give your proposal a lot of thought, Stanley. I don't want to do anything that interferes with a proper and ethical arrangement between a lawyer and his client, but I recognize how effective your solution to the hustling problem is in your own courtroom. I agree this unethical solicitation by lawyers hanging around our buildings gives a tawdry veneer to our whole profession, so I will have to think about it. Have a nice day. You'll hear from me soon."

Two days later, Judge Casper received a Transfer of Assignment memorandum in the mail from Judge Largo, which read:

"Effective immediately, you are transferred to the Gun Court situated in Building One of the Cabrini Green Housing Project. The proliferation of guns at that project continues with increasing frequency. I have every confidence your innovative ways will improve the climate there."

Regards,
Presiding Judge Henry Largo

After reading the memorandum, Judge Casper expressed his revulsion at the transfer order. Ain't this a bitch, he thought. I gave him a foolproof way to clean up the branch courts and the traffic court and restore some professional ethics to the practice of law there, and what does Judge Largo do? He ignores my suggestion about not approving CBRs and then dispatches me to the hell hole of the Cabrini Green Gun Court so that I will be buried there forever. There is not one word about not approving CBRs for the regulars and with me disappearing in the bowels of Cabrini Green, nobody will be the wiser. A great way to start your stewardship, Judge Largo. ⚖

Operation Greylord initially concentrated on the Criminal Court Building because of the information supplied by Rex Reed. Reed's practice centered on those types of cases, and the judges and staff he knew about became fertile targets for suspicion and targeting. The results of the U.S. Attorney's concentration on criminal matters, including those cases assigned to branch courts, were proving highly successful to this point, even as much work remained.

Buoyed by the results to date, U.S. Attorney Hartnett thought the time was right to consider expansion of Operation Greylord to the civil side of the Cook County Court system. There had been many rumors about a particular judge assigned to the Chancery Division of the court who, allegedly, engaged in some highly unusual conduct in some of his cases. The Chancery Division was the most important division of the civil side and was designed to hear the more complex cases. The judges in Chancery were empowered to award equitable (non-monetary) relief to the prevailing parties in addition to monetary awards. Assignment to that division was highly prized and sought after among all the judges in the system.

Although rumors were worthless in a court of law, depending on their sources and frequency of repetition, it was foolhardy to ignore them as a possible starting point in an investigatory exploration. Such was the state of affairs with Judge Ruben Jordas, about whom swirled a good deal of head scratching. Although Reed could offer no first-hand specifics about any illegal conduct on the part of Jordas and no first-hand experience in his court, Reed heard plenty of stories about Jordas and his conduct in his in-chambers off-the-record conferences with lawyers appearing before him.

First Assistant U.S. Attorney Ben Jones and AUSA Dan Hogan were asked to meet with Hartnett to discuss the expansion of Operation Greylord to the civil side of the Circuit Court of Cook County and, in particular, Judge Ruben Jordas.

"Good morning, gentlemen," greeted Hartnett. "How is our investigation going?"

"About as good as we had hoped," responded Hogan. "We've had a couple of sticky situations where one of our undercover agents pretending to be a participant in a bar fight got himself arrested. The judge set a high bond, which took us awhile to get approval to get the cash and post it. Our guy wound up spending some very unpleasant time in jail before he got out."

"Anything happen to him while he was in?" asked Hartnett. "Apparently word got to the tier he was locked up in that he was supposed to be some tough guy; I guess because he was in for aggravated battery. A couple of guys lodged in the same tier wanted to take on our agent and test his manhood and see how tough he really was. We had to pull some fast strings to get him released before things got out of hand," said Hogan.

"I hope the pulled strings don't wind up unraveling the whole shebang."

"I think we're OK, but honestly, there is always a risk, said Hogan. Jones added, "I'm pretty sure we're OK. We didn't use any members of the judiciary to get the release, and it was all done low key."

"What I wanted to broach with the two of you is an expansion of the investigation. There can't be much doubt that some of this corruption has crept over to the civil side, and there is so much conversation swirling around one guy who sits on that side that it's hard to ignore. Do either of you know who I'm referring to?" asked Hartnett.

"I've probably heard some of the same stuff you're referring to. Is it about Judge Ruben Jordas?" asked Jones.

"He's the one, all right. What have you heard?"

"Well, for one thing, he's supposed to be as shrewd as can be. I have not heard of him taking payoffs directly, but he has these unusual ways of generating money which winds up with him," offered Jones.

"What do you mean?"

"One method I heard goes like this. He portrays his wife as a gifted artist who hasn't been discovered yet but who will be acknowledged someday as one of the greatest artists of the day. He talks about her at the drop of a hat. His chambers is adorned with her work hanging on the walls; when lawyers go in there for pretrial conferences, it's show and tell time. He spends more time telling the lawyers about what inspired each painting and what feature gives it a status that will be universally recognized for its uniqueness and value, than he spends discussing the case the lawyers are appearing on and how to solve their differences."

"I've heard about the same thing," said Hartnett.

Jones then added, "The guy is a real salesman. The next thing you know, these lawyers are asking if the pieces are for sale and, if so, for how much. I even heard that a bidding war broke out in the open once when he said they were all for sale."

"Has any responsible art critic or expert ever supported the idea of Jordas' wife's genius?" asked Hartnett.

"Not that I've ever heard," answered Jones.

"So, what's the rest of the story?"

Jones continued, "The rumors are that the lawyers who succeed in buying his wife's art are often successful in how they do when the judge decides their cases. You know, in certain civil cases, juries are rarely employed and the presiding judge has all the decision-making power. These court cases are ripe for misadventure."

"Do you have a proposal? How should we proceed?" asked Hogan. Jones responded, "The obvious problem in prosecuting the scheme I described is two-fold. One is the intervention of the wife and payments intended for her and not the judge. The other problem arises as to what any painting is worth. If the paintings are viewed as valueless, then the argument that a lawyer buying worthless art from the wife of a judge overseeing his case can be seen for the apparent sham it appears to be. But if there is a genuine and bona fide difference of opinion over the value of the painting bought, a pissing contest over the worth of the painting will obscure what we will contend is really a sham transaction. The facts become muddled and instead of having a clean quid pro quo, we are in the world of art and the true worth of paintings. And given what they sometimes sell for, who is to say what the worth of any painting really is?"

"Any trial like that will be reduced to the word of different experts. The art world has never been a black and white measure of things. There is no objectivity to be found, and our theory of valueless art will remain just that—a theory instead of cold, hard facts," said Hogan.

Hartnett then said, "Another way I heard Jordas likes to operate is to tout his wife's insurance selling powers, something she does when she's not painting masterpieces."

"So how does this one work?"

Hartnett continued, "This one is much simpler. When the judge is discussing the case with the lawyers back in chambers—and it's important that these are chambers' conversations with no court reporter present who records the conversations taking place—the topic of insurance is inevitably raised. Everyone agrees that you can never have enough insurance, so the judge has a nice opening to let everybody know about the fact that his wife is an independent insurance agent specializing in plans for lawyers and law firms, large or small."

"You're kidding. Does he shill for his wife with a straight face? Between painting and hustling insurance, the poor lady must never sleep," Hogan cynically suggested.

"She must stay awake all night just counting her money," volunteered Jones.

Hartnett then said, "Although this one seems more straight forward, especially if the lawyer buying insurance did not need any and was not in the market looking to buy, all of a sudden realizes he doesn't have quite enough coverage and doesn't want to pass up the opportunity to buy more."

"Unless the wife is gouging these guys price-wise, it sounds like another pissing contest about ulterior motives on the part of the buyer.

To make a criminal case, we'll have to show a strong correlation between the lawyers' insurance purchases and successes in getting favorable rulings from the judge," said Jones.

"I see what you mean about shrewd. There must be a cleaner way we can make a case against a judge like this than getting into art or insurance issues," said Hogan, already contemplating how the case should be presented to a jury.

"I propose we try to get one of our made-up cases assigned to him with our undercover people. It may be that Jordas is so confident in how he structures these payments, he might propose something to lawyers he does not even know and has not had any prior dealings with. He may think disguising payments this way is so foolproof that he'll chance it with one of our lawyers," proposed Jones.

"I wholeheartedly agree, said Hartnett. "There are probably ethical issues involved in pitching his wife's services this way, but our interest goes much deeper than ethics. It may be that his conversations with the lawyers directly reflect a correlation between the case he is hearing and what he is pitching to the lawyers."

"I agree. A guy this greedy and, apparently, this successful with using his wife this way may get sloppy in his conduct and say things that directly links his judicial conduct and business with his wife," surmised Hogan.

Summarizing the discussion, Hartnett said, "Let's do it. Put some thoughts together on an appropriate case to file in Civil Court so we can get it in front of him. We will then see face-to-face what he's really made of. Meanwhile, we'll look at the roster of lawyers who appear before him regularly and appear to benefit from his rulings in any way, particularly in appointments as receivers or trustees over entities or projects with significant fees being paid out." ⚖

In accordance with the discussion, Jones, Hogan and a group of assigned undercover FBI agents created the fictional case of Michigan Avenue Property Owners v. 494 N. Michigan Ave. Inc. Although acting undercover, the agents were, in fact, real lawyers. Consistent with federal law permitting the secret transmission and recording of conversations in which one party to the conversation consents to the recording (all the undercover agents here), each of the undercover agents was wearing a wire. The case was assigned to Judge Ruben Jordas. Transcripts of all the conversations were later prepared, and this is how they read.

Courtroom Deputy: Hear Ye, Hear Ye, Hear Ye. All who have business before the court shall draw near and will be heard, Judge Ruben Jordas presiding. The Court calls the case of: Michigan Avenue Property Owners v. 494 N. Michigan Avenue, Inc., Case No. 82 C 303.

Hardy: Good Morning, Your Honor. William Hardy for the Plaintiff.

Sierra: Good Morning, Your Honor. Sam Sierra for the Defendant.

Jordas: Good Morning, Gentlemen. I believe this is the first appearance for this case, is it not?

Hardy: Yes, Judge, you are correct. The Complaint was filed one month ago, and the Defendant was served right away. The Defendant has answered. So the case is at issue. We are anxious to proceed because the Plaintiffs are being damaged daily as the status quo continues.

Sierra: The Defendant takes exception to the argument of counsel, especially coming before we even had a chance to tell you what the case is about.

Jordas: Just relax, gentlemen, There will be time enough later for advocacy, but right now I would like brief presentations from each of you as to what the case is about and your respective positions in it. We'll start with Plaintiff's Counsel. You may proceed accordingly, Mr. Hardy.

Hardy: Thank you, Your Honor. The Plaintiffs in this case consist of approximately 50 residential condominium owners in a forty story high-rise building on North Michigan Avenue in Chicago. Anyone familiar with what is called "The Magnificent Mile" has probably passed the building dozens of times. It is a fairly new building, and it is a mixed use complex. The first 5 floors are devoted to commercial space with the other 35 floors devoted to residential condominiums of varying sizes. The 5 floors of commercial space and all of the common areas of the other 35 floors are owned by the defendant.

Hardy shows the court a picture of the building.

Hardy: The condos are all privately owned by various unrelated parties, and they have all joined together to bring this lawsuit. The nub of the lawsuit is the fact that the Defendant has been lax and inefficient in its management and leasing obligations of the five floors of the commercial space, and its failure to do better is costing my clients to suffer considerable financial penalties as a result.

Jordas: How so?

Hardy: The consequences to my clients are twofold, Your Honor. First, as written in all the contracts for the sale of the condominiums, each condo owner is obligated to pay a maintenance fee to the defendant for its management of the commercial space and its maintenance of the common areas of the other 35 floors. Those fees are substantial, and the only way they can be reduced is when the commercial space is either fully leased or substantially so. So irrespective of whether the Defendant is a good leasing agent, my clients are paying out the nose, good or bad. The second hit to my clients is the high cost of maintenance for the commercial space when it is vacant as opposed to when the space is leased. When the space is leased out, the responsibility and costs of maintenance are passed on to the lessee. When the space is vacant, in effect, my clients pay the cost of maintenance, which is also higher than when the space is occupied. That is why, Your Honor, we have asked for the appointment of a receiver for the five floors of commercial space and the common areas as soon as possible. This is a wonderful building with desirable space, and it is only because of the ineptitude of the Defendant that my clients are bearing a burden they never anticipated and which reduces the joy of living where they do. Thank you very much.

Jordas: I'll hear from the Defendant.

Sierra: Thank you, Your Honor. I must start off, unexpectedly so, where my opponent left off, having to do with his clients' expectations and anticipations. In each of his client's contracts, written in plain English and in plain view on the first page, their obligations to pay the fees they are now complaining about is set forth. Only the ignorant or the blind could not see or understand the obligations set forth in each of the contracts of purchase. As for the charge of ineptitude, I dare say a good number of counsel's clients are probably sophisticated business people and, perhaps, investors in the market.

Sierra holds up a copy of a contract.

Anyone with the least sensitivity to the fluctuations of the marketplace, particularly real estate and commercial retail operations, would have an appreciation for the tough times we have all been through for the last five years. Down markets affect us all, not only the lazy and slothful, but the able and energetic. It is in my client's own interest to find tenants for this highly desirable space in the building he constructed and in which he constantly seeks to maximize its benefits. The world of immediate and complete gratification exists only among those who daydream through life, oblivious to the tides of change, and blinded by their own selfish desires.

Hardy: Your Honor, excuse me for interrupting, but Counsel's suggestion that my clients inhabit a fanciful world disconnected from reality is both offensive and inaccurate, and I resent it.

Jordas: Relax, Counsel. At this stage, it is excused rhetoric and does not constitute evidence in the case. Did you finish your presentation, Mr. Sierra?

Sierra: The last point I wanted to make, Your Honor, is that the relief he is requesting, the appointment of a receiver, is both extraordinary and, in truth, self-defeating. Any professional receiver worthy of appointment would come at a substantial cost. Fees for that outside appointment, I suggest, would have to be borne by his clients, one way or another, in addition to depriving my client of fees he is contractually entitled to receive. Instead of making things better, they would only get worse if we were to follow his suggestion. Thank you very much.

Jordas: Well, I see that both counsel feel quite strongly about their positions in this case, dare I even say emotional. It has long been my experience in these matters that cases so polarized at their inception are prime candidates for exploration of the possibility of settlement. There is much to be gained, especially by the parties, for an early end to highly disputed matters. The second thing my long experience suggests to me is to speak to each side informally in the absence of the other side to see if mutually agreed terms can be reached to avoid the great expense of protracted proceedings. I can only engage in the latter way with the agreement of the parties since ex-parte conversations are, as you both know, prohibited. Mr. Hardy, do you have any objection to meeting with me alone and then my meeting with your adversary alone? It is often the way most conducive to candor with the court and an emphasis on what can be agreed upon as opposed to what divides you. Any objection, Mr. Hardy?

Hardy: None at all, Judge. It's a good idea.

Jordas: Mr. Sierra?

Sierra: I agree Judge, it's a good idea. Who do you want to see first?

Jordas: I think I'll start with Plaintiffs' counsel, Mr. Hardy. We'll meet in my chambers. Follow me, Mr. Hardy.

Whereupon, Judge Jordas and William Hardy proceeded to Judge Jordas' chambers; they were the only two present.

Jordas: Tell me, Mr. Hardy, are your own clients all lathered up about this?

Hardy: You probably know how it is when you have a group together. You have a firebrand or two, wanting to tar and feather the other side, another bunch who agree with the common position espoused, but who are much more rational in their thought process. Then you have the last bunch, who are much more patient with building management, but have to get along with all their neighbors and don't want to be seen as unsupportive of the majority view.

Jordas: How many would you say you have to satisfy, whatever position you might adopt?

Hardy: There are probably two I have to appease. One thing is helpful to me, they are the ones who hired me and know me best. So I carry some influence with the leaders.

Jordas: One of the problems I have in trying to find a middle ground between both sides is your demand for a receiver. I mean, at some point, I will have to bite the bullet and either appoint one or deny the request for appointment. If the dispute was only about money, you have much more room to operate and money can always be divided. Not so with a receiver. Unlike King Solomon, I cannot decree that I shall cut the receiver in half and give you only half. So you see, that avenue is not open to me to suggest as a compromise. But I do have another idea.

Hardy: What is that, Your Honor? You have a reputation for inventive solutions, so we're kind of lucky we got you on the assignment.

Jordas: A possible solution might be to give you a whole receiver, but not yet. I think the real estate market and the economy on which it depends is starting to turn around, so it may be wise to give the defendant a certain period of time to achieve an agreed level of occupancy in the space. If they don't achieve that, then, with both sides in agreement, I can select a receiver to take over the leasing function. I've had lots of cases in the past where I have had to appoint one kind of receiver or another, so I have a whole stable of them at the ready. These appointments turn out to be pretty lucrative, so they are more than anxious to get the appointments. What do you think of that idea?

Hardy: It sounds like it has some promise. Obviously, the two variables in your suggestion, aside from the identity of the receiver which we could leave to you, is the length of time to give the defendant to sign up the space, and the percentage of occupancy which would be satisfactory under the terms which would be negotiated.

Jordas: I quite agree those two things would be the key to any deal. I guess what I'm asking you is, if we can reach agreement on those two things, would you sign on to that structure of settlement this early in the game? Would you strongly recommend it to your clients?

Hardy: It sure sounds like a way out, and it would save my clients and the defendant a whole lot of money. Assuming agreement on those two items, I could go for it.

Jordas: That's great. It's a major first step. Now let me chat with your opponent and see if he is as forthcoming.

William Hardy left the room and Sam Sierra entered the room.

Sierra: Judge, we sure handed you a tough one. My client is really aggravated with these people. He puts up a nice building, sells most of the units in short order on reasonable terms, accommodates their special desires and needs, and before we get a reasonable chance to get some good commercial tenants in there instead of some fly by night outfits, they're all bitching because we haven't moved fast enough. Ingrates, all.

Jordas: I know what you mean about needing time to put the pieces in place to get something going in the right way.

Sierra: I'm glad you appreciate that. We originally concentrated on selling the condos, and we did that in record time. After that is when we concentrated on the commercial space. That takes time, and we wanted to make sure any commercial tenants were acceptable to the condo owners because we view the building as one integrated operation. We wanted their input and for them to be happy with what goes in there. After all, they are the best potential customers. We barely started with that and, instead of thanking us for being thoughtful and taking time to do it right, they greet us with this goddamn lawsuit. Some thanks. See what I mean?

Jordas: I know very well what you mean, Sam. My wife has recently started a project close to her heart, and it has taken much longer than she thought it would to get it off the ground. The red tape is endless and getting the right people and organizations to get behind it is a lot tougher than you would think, especially given its purpose.

Sierra: What is it, may I ask?

Jordas: Of course. She feels very strongly that of all the health issues in America, the most devastating is cancer. It destroys so many lives and kills so randomly, and progress toward an attempted cure so slow and so seemingly unattainable, it's maddening.

Sierra: God forbid that she has it.

Jordas: No, she's lucky. Neither she nor anyone in our immediate family has fallen victim to it. She decided to devote her skill and energies to its eradication and since she is only a layperson, she thinks the most effective thing she can do is raise money toward its cure. After all, who doesn't want to put an end to it?

Sierra: Good for her, if she has the time, energy, and passion to do something. It sounds like she does.

Jordas: Our kids are grown now, and for a good while she took up painting as a hobby. She had some other business interests but gave them up and also quit painting to devote full time to her new pursuit.

Sierra: Is she just getting started then? At least like my client did, she doesn't have to build a building.

Jordas: No, she doesn't have to do that, but she is building something else. She formed a tax-exempt organization and finally got IRS approval for it. People can now make contributions to it and are able to get a tax deduction for what they contribute. Lots of red tape there. Now she has to get the right people to staff it, others to publicize it, and get it moving. You may or may not have any idea how much competition there is out there for contributions, even as worthy a cause as killing cancer is.

Sierra: How is she doing now that she is properly organized?

Jordas: She's doing OK, but it's pretty much of a one-person band at this point. These charities have to raise X amount of money just to cover operating expenses—you know, salaries and rent, etc. Only then can they turn over the rest to the researchers and doctors. That is what she is about, and she can use all the contributions that come her way.

Sierra: I'm sure my client would like to contribute to a worthy cause like your wife's. Do you think that would be OK, I mean, considering where we are?

Jordas: I'm sure it's OK, since it involves just her and not me. But if he decided to do something it would probably be best until this case was over. I mean I'm sure it's all cricket under the rules, but why give anybody something to talk about.

Sierra: I know what you mean and I agree with you. I'm sure my client will be generous to her cause.

Jordas: I appreciate it. Do you have some idea of how much time your client would like to work on the leasing of the space?

Sierra: I think he would like two years but could probably live with one year. As for the occupancy rate, I think the level that is fair to both sides would be 80%. What do you think, Judge?

Jordas: I think both positions are reasonable, so let me see if I can get the other side to agree. Let me have you switch seats one more time.

Sam Sierra then left the chambers and William Hardy returned.

Hardy: So how did it go, Judge?

Jordas: To my pleasant surprise, your opponent signed on. Of course, I had to pressure him on the two open items of importance, the length of time his client could have to lease the space and what rate of occupancy is satisfactory. I didn't think you would agree to two years, so I told him I'd only suggest one year; he thought he could sell that. As for occupancy, I told him it had to be at least 80%. He balked at that, but I told him that 80% was a reasonable criterion for success in that field, and I would not recommend anything below that. I had to twist his arm a little, but finally got agreement as to both. So the defendant has one year to get 80% occupancy or at least a contractual commitment. If he fails to do that, I appoint a receiver of my choice. Is that a deal?

Hardy: Judge, you've got a deal. ⚖

A meeting in U.S. Attorney Hartnett's office was scheduled for the next afternoon. Jones and Hogan, having monitored the interception of all the conversations the undercover agents had with Judge Jordas, would debrief the agents that morning.

Hartnett said, "Good morning, gentlemen. I'm anxious to hear about the case before Judge Jordas."

Jones responded, "It went very well, Brandon. The agents first appeared in open court and then went back to chambers for a settlement conference. Jordas did not make any overtures to the plaintiffs' lawyer, but when he got the defense lawyer back there—he talked to each side separately—he opened up about his wife and her new, cancer-fighting, charitable corporation. He said getting contributions are vital to getting it off the ground and pretty much invited the defense lawyer to do so."

Hartnett asked, "What else did he say? Did he acknowledge there might be problems presiding over a case which, in the midst of, his wife receives a sizable contribution for her new charity from one of the parties to the case?"

Jones answered, "He sure enough acknowledged that wouldn't look good, and perhaps any contribution should be made when the case was over. Then he went about settling the case, at least as between the lawyers, by pretending to exert some force on the defense lawyer regarding terms which he urged the plaintiff's lawyer to take, since they were better for the plaintiff than the defense was initially prepared to offer. He bragged to the plaintiffs' lawyer about twisting defense counsel's arm to make a decent offer to the plaintiff when, in truth, defense counsel offered the terms on his own. He didn't have to be forced to do so by the judge."

Hartnett then asked, shaking his head, "So you're saying that Jordas is not only a crook but a liar as well?"

"You're not surprised, are you?"

Hogan added, "That man is one smooth operator. From using his wife as an artist, insurance broker, and now cancer fighter, there seems to be no end to what she's capable of doing. Jordas must stay up nights thinking up this stuff."

Hartnett then asked, "Have you done any homework on her new charity?"

Jones responded, "Sure have. It's only about two and a half years old, and IRS was good enough to give us copies of the only two returns it has filed."

"What's the company's name?"

Jones said, "It is Yes, We Cancure Cancer, or "YWCC". Pretty catchy, huh? One letter removed from YWCA, which everyone recognizes. Maybe that's intentional?"

Hartnett said, "You think? Nothing Jordas does is without thought and reason."

Jones added, "And not without personal benefit. Here's the structure: the wife is Chairman of the Board and President. The other two board members are in show business; no medical people sit on the board. Board members are not paid, and they only get reimbursed for expenses."

"What does the staff look like?" asked Hogan.

Jones replied, "There is only one employee who, naturally, does everything that is needed to get done. Her salary is set at $50,000 a year, with a bonus at the discretion of the President. No bonuses have been paid yet."

"What about the President's compensation?" asked Hogan.

"It is set at $150,000 per year, plus bonuses when able," responded Jones.

"What does the charity show as income so far?"

"The first year it applied for a grant from the State of Illinois and received $50,000 in grant money for research. Private contributions were a little over $50,000, so the first year's income was used entirely for the two salaries, with the President being owed the balance of her salary she did not receive."

"What about the second year?"

Jones continued, "There was no state grant the second year, only private contributions of almost $150,000."

"What were the disbursements?"

Jones answered. "All of the income went to salary, with the President getting most of it. Their only employee quit at the end of the second year because she had not been paid what had been promised in either the first or second year. She has not been replaced."

"I take it that none of the income was ever forwarded to others or used in any way for research or any other medical purpose. Is that so?" asked Hartnett.

"No chance of that." answered Jones.

Hartnett thought aloud, "Well, if we wanted something more blatant and straight forward, that's what we got."

Hogan, playing devil's advocate, said, "Of course, the argument is that the newness of the enterprise and getting fully operational takes a lot of time. They will say paying it all out in salaries, mostly to the President, is necessary seed money for success in the future."

Jones answered, "The comeback to that is to cut down on salaries and pay what you can afford, not to just give it to the Mrs. and not use a penny of it for the purpose set out in the corporate charter."

Hogan, nodding in agreement, "Right on. Let Jordas sing that tune to a jury, even while he introduces the idea of making contributions by lawyers who are appearing before him and who are dependent on his fairness and integrity for getting a fair shake in his rulings."

"I agree, offered Hartnett. "The judge's position—and his wife's—will not play well with any discerning jury. Who won't be able to see through that charade, especially if we can get evidence of the artwork sales and her insurance commissions into evidence?"

Jones then remarked, "In case we needed something even stronger at trial, I should tell you about the other prong of the investigation. We've previously discussed how the opportunity to appoint receivers of companies in a variety of circumstances is a fairly common occurrence.

Many of those appointments are lucrative, even when the companies they are appointed for are in bad financial straits. This is so, because, in these cases the receivers always get their fees first. Their money comes off the top, before you get down to the creditors of the business or even the employees. They are just like bankruptcy cases."

"I assume you have talked to some of those receivers," said Hartnett.

"We have," answered Jones. "And, as we expected, Jordas regularly uses a certain few."

"I'll bet these guys get rattled easily, don't they?" asked Hartnett.

"Our experience is that at the first sign of trouble, some go right to criminal defense lawyers before they talk to us. There is lots of potential evidence out there," replied Jones.

Hogan asked, "Have you confirmed anything yet?"

Jones replied, "As Brandon knows, we made a deal with one of his regularly appointed receivers—it's an informal agreement, but binding nonetheless—who told us what he has done in the past and what he is expected to do when he is appointed in the future. He is a talented lawyer and does a good job, but talent only takes you so far with our good judge."

Hogan asked, "How much do the appointments cost, and how does he pay?"

"The man says the kickbacks run about 10% of what he collects in fees, and they are always made in cash. It's just like spy stuff; limited phone contacts and clandestine meetings," responded Jones.

"How many payments has he made to date?" pressed Hogan, already thinking about an argument to the jury.

"About five, and the total is somewhere close to $100,000," answered Jones.

"I assume no other witnesses can corroborate the payments?" Hogan asked, still thinking of a future trial.

"No one else. But the guy is as meticulous as can be, and he has created a record-keeping system documenting all the payments, all of his withdrawals, dates, times, and locations of meetings. Although they are his own records, he comes across as not only precise and accurate, but believable," asserted Jones.

Hogan, wearing a look of approval, said, "Guys like that do well on the stand and even if they get a pass on criminal prosecution, it is a small price to pay for what they give us. They're worth their weight in gold."

Hartnett then added, "When you couple the testimony of direct bribe payments with all of the indirect stuff going through the wife, I believe a jury can readily see through the machinations. Even with the wife, Judge Jordas is the instrumentality for getting the money into her hands."

Hogan, still pleased, said, "I guess wearing the robe allows you to be a marketing genius to benefit your wife and a judicial genius to benefit litigants. Two for the price of one."

"It's all coming together, boys. Nice going, Hartnett said approvingly. ⚖

Just as the 1976 national election saw a change in the party of the president-elect, so too did the 1980 Presidential election. Brandon Hartnett, as was customary, tendered his resignation in January 1981 to the new president. Operation Greylord was in full swing with the change of administration, however, and the successful results to-date precluded a reevaluation of the need for it or the methods employed. There would be no hastily arranged meeting with a new Attorney General for the purpose of justifying the investigation again in light of the proven results.

The U.S. Attorney's office in Chicago had, throughout the 1970s, established itself as the premier law enforcement office in the area. Under the outstanding leadership of a series of United States Attorneys, there were no sacred cows that were off limits to the discerning eyes of law enforcement agents. As a result, there was no shortage of highly qualified applicants for the position of United States Attorney in Chicago in early 1981.

By virtue of his extraordinary success as an Assistant U.S. Attorney during the early 1970s, the candidacy of Jeffrey Michaels made him a leading choice to head the office he once started in as a novice. While an Assistant, Michaels had been assigned to a succession of first-chair responsibilities of increasing importance and difficulty and came to be known as the "go to" guy in the office. Michaels was universally recognized as the best trial lawyer in an office of excellent trial lawyers, and nobody begrudged the recognition and fame which came his way.

Jeffrey Michaels was appointed the United States Attorney for the Northern District of Illinois in early 1981. Michaels' succession as a replacement for Brandon Hartnett in the Operation Greylord investigation was seamless. There was considerable work remaining to be done against a number of targets, including Judge John Lunden.

The lid of secrecy of Operation Greylord was lifted when separate multi-count indictments were returned against a number of judges, other court officials, police officers and private lawyers. Included among the judges were John Lunden and Sam Wilson. The charges included, among others, receiving or paying bribes to fix the outcome of hundreds of cases, from drunk driving to the possession with intent to distribute drugs, to battery, and to theft.

Roger Flynn was among the private lawyers indicted. The criminal charges against Flynn and Wilson were based mainly on tape recorded conversations, wiretapped interceptions of private conversations, and other evidence supplied by Peter Theos.

As for Roger Flynn, his indictment left Theos with mixed emotions. First and foremost among them was the professional satisfaction which comes from doing your public service job well and, in a real sense, protecting the institutions of government and justice which serve all citizens. Respect for the law is not, and cannot simply be, an empty slogan. Who knows how much harm to society can be wrought when a criminal can buy his freedom and continue to prey on citizens rather than being made to pay for his past crimes. That includes lawyers who corruptly help bring about those opportunities.

The other hard-to-dispel emotion on Theos' part regarding Flynn was the friendship and kindness he often provided to Theos. Those things reflected the truth among many law violators. Even crooks can possess admirable human qualities and characteristics. The effect on Flynn's family was difficult to ponder.

Theos' reaction to Wilson's indictment reflected much less sympathy than for Flynn. Wilson was a judge, a higher and more influential rank than a lawyer. Wilson's capacity for evil and wrongdoing far exceeded that of Flynn's and the ensuing harm to society more profound.

The public surprise which accompanied the return of the indictments was a testament to the Government's ability to keep its investigation a secret. Beyond surprise on the public's part, however, was the shock and dismay which accompanied the news. The apparent widespread basis of the judicial corruption exposed was difficult to comprehend and impossible to accept. As the cases worked their way through the federal criminal justice system, meaningful reform would have to await the process.

U.S. Attorney Jeffrey Michaels would personally try the Lunden case along with Dan Hogan, the most knowledgeable assistant on Greylord and the most able. Judge Lunden and his retained counsel, Michael McGrath, were quite emphatic in their protestations of innocence and said they looked forward to a trial by a jury of Judge Lunden's peers. McGrath ran a small office of seasoned criminal defense lawyers, all of whom enjoyed excellent reputations.

The extensive investigation by the Government produced an enormous amount of discovery material to be provided to the defense, including recorded interviews. A trial date was set six months from Judge Lunden's plea of not guilty, a period deemed acceptable by both sides. Pretrial preparations were undertaken in earnest, with perhaps the most important decision to be made by the Government was the use of Moe Sands as a witness against Lunden. The debate raged for days within the office and, in the end, the choice was to call Sands to corroborate the bribe payment lawyer Spencer gave Lunden.

The Government's evidence was reviewed, assessed, rereviewed, and reassessed. There were no illusions about the first judge case to go to trial in Greylord; it would be a bellwether case. The great unknown would be how a jury of citizens would view serious charges of criminality lodged against an otherwise respected public figure who rose through the legal and political ranks to a position of prominence.

In addition to the Moe Sands' bribe money, evidence of some Miracle Workers giving bagmen lists of cases they were handling in which they desired favorable outcomes for their clients, along with sealed envelopes for the judge, were on the agenda. When prosecutors went against these miracle workers, they rarely won, but when prosecutors went against public defenders, prosecutors won 90% of the time. No logical explanation could justify the differential, and it is a certainty that some clients of public defenders, innocent though they may have been, were convicted in order to balance the statistical outcome of cases.

There were other little tidbits in the Government's arsenal, but this was the lion's share of their proof. There was, of course, the incident of a female client of a miracle worker who admitted on cross-examination she could feel the beers she drank, followed by a direction to the miracle worker from Judge Lunden that "he better speak with his client" during a break. The "not guilty" verdict came without explanation.

The expected favorable character evidence of Judge Lunden would allow the introduction of anti-character evidence, particularly from prosecutors who lost in virtually every case they had against the miracle workers. The testimony from particular bagmen would supply the reasons for those losses but would not eradicate the anger over how and why prosecutors lost those cases.

As for the defense case, it was not expected that the defense would present any significant amount of new material to learn and become familiar with for use at trial. It was almost a certainty that Lunden would testify on his own behalf and deny all the misconduct hurled his way. Because some of the conversations he had in chambers with undercover agents or lawyers were recorded, their importance would be exalted because of the recordings.

The trial itself reflected vigorous advocacy on all sides. The conduct on the part of all the lawyers, although impassioned at times, nevertheless stayed within the bounds of professionalism. Because the Government had the burden of proof, its lawyers were permitted to argue both first and last to the jury, even as the amount of time allowed to address the jury was the same for both sides for final argument. Following, in part, was the presentation made by United States Attorney Jeffrey Michaels.

"Ladies and Gentlemen of the Jury. Your presence here today, as well as your vital role in this case, originated thousands of years ago. The jury system has been honed through the years and has stood the test of time as one of the most fundamental, and most vital, methods of how civilizations govern themselves in their most important obligations; the rendition of justice to one and all. The birth of the jury system took place in a small country in Europe called Hellas, now known as Greece. It came during the period known as the "cradle of civilization," a time when noble ideas flourished and were adopted as principles worthy of our devotion.

"Another of the ideas then proclaimed and which we still revere is that man is fit to govern himself, that there is none among us who has a special birthright and can claim power by virtue of it. Simply stated, all men and women are created equal.

"The history of democracy in America and the continued vitality of the jury system is predicated on the fundamental decency, capacity, and fairness of the members of the community we all come from. When juries apply their powers of reason, where no juror has any special interest in the outcome of the case, and when each juror is committed to applying the same level of objectivity to the evidence that they would wish for themselves, when settled principles of law are accepted and followed, the collective result—the jury verdicts—are unassailable. The passage of 2,500 years in which jurors like yourselves have rendered verdicts in millions of cases, both criminal and civil, has proved the wisdom of the concept. The justice produced in that way has never been equaled by any other method in any other civilization.

"Compare this system of justice to the system of justice employed by the defendant when he was dispensing justice in the Circuit Court of Cook County. The only principle employed by him can be simply stated. The credo was simply: "Where's Mine."

"Who won or lost was determined by that old Chicago proverb,

"What's in it for me?" You have all seen, at some time or another, a statue of Lady Justice and the empty scales of justice before her, her eyes bound so that she cannot be influenced by the identities or interests of the parties before her. Her scales are empty of evidence and balanced evenly, awaiting only the quantity and quality of evidence to be put thereon so she can decide the case. Lady Justice represents the ideal—the way verdicts are to be arrived at, blind to the identity of the litigants and oblivious to any inequalities among them by virtue of their fortunes in life. Now that is the way you and I would visualize the Lady Justice depiction, blind to everything about the case other than its merits, determined by the weight of the evidence and the applicable law. How do you think this judge defendant viewed her? This defendant, and others like him, say the blindfold covering Lady Justice's eyes render her as being unable to see the illegal cash the defendant was stuffing into his pockets—hidden from the view of justice and all those citizens who believed in the concepts of honesty and integrity."

"I want to thank you for your service in this case. I am confident that you will do the right thing."

Defense Counsel then began his final argument. A portion of it reads as follows, "Ladies and Gentlemen of the Jury, I too want to thank you for your service in this case. We are also appreciative of the time you have devoted to judging the life and conduct of my client, depicted as he is by the might of the federal government and all the powers at its disposal. Judge Lunden stands equal before the law and, indeed, is clothed with the protection all who are similarly accused enjoy. It is a principle of law, as important as the jury system itself, that Judge Lunden is presumed innocent of all the charges against him. He doesn't have to prove his innocence, the law bestows that on him. And before you may find him guilty, each of you, all of you, must become convinced of his guilt of the charges beyond a reasonable doubt, a very high standard indeed.

"And what does the Government rely on to prove that? Is it the word of common, upstanding, hardworking citizens? Hardly. The Government has paraded before you drug dealers, crooked lawyers, bagmen for other crooked parties, and other ne'er do wells. Is that the quality of evidence that should be relied on to overcome the presumption of innocence?

"It was through the dint of hard work that my client worked his way through law school to become a lawyer. It was also through hard work, and demonstrated skill, that he rose in the ranks of lawyers to be appointed and then elected a judge. Compare the quality of man he is in contrast to all the crooks who testified for the Government.

Thank you very much."

Assistant U.S. Attorney Dan Hogan then delivered his brief rebuttal argument. "Ladies and Gentlemen of the Jury, ask yourselves how all of the Government witnesses who are now castigated came to appear in this case. They were here as witnesses because Judge Lunden chose them all—he chose them, in spite of their character, because they were willing to put money in his pocket, lots of money. From hundreds to thousands of dollars, these are the people he chose to do his illegal business with. The good guys would not have stuffed bribes into his pocket; that's why they are not here as witnesses. It was these creeps Judge Lunden favored. Some of the verdicts he issued were laughable. They were not the product of evidence but the product of cash. With Judge Lunden, cash was king, not evidence. Thank you very much."

The jury was then instructed and began deliberations for the balance of the afternoon. They recessed and returned the following morning to resume their deliberations. Shortly before noon and after all the lawyers and parties were assembled, the jury returned the following verdict in open court. "We the jury, find the Defendant, John Lunden, guilty as charged." ⚖

The return of guilty verdicts on all counts in the case of United States of America vs. John Lunden, the first judge defendant to go to trial in Operation Greylord, produced sighs of relief in the Dirksen Federal Courthouse offices of the United States Attorney and the Federal Bureau of Investigation. When the initial indictments of some low-level operatives in the corruption alleged were returned some of the methods used by the Government were disclosed.

During the joint investigation by the U.S. Attorney's office and the FBI, a firm belief in the propriety of the undercover methods employed was held by all the personnel working on the cases. Nevertheless, their outward expressions of confidence in the legality of their methods and the strength of the evidence produced thereby was, at times, simply camouflage for the fear that juries of common men and women empaneled to decide the cases might not agree.

It was one thing for the law to sanction the investigators' conduct. It was a separate and different proposition as to whether the public at large would accept the idea that not only was the undercover conduct lawful, but fair and just in its usage to ferret out corruption. At the least, the guilty verdicts put to rest, for the moment, the necessity for the employment of the Government's deceit against corrupt, but unwitting, public officials.

Rather than the jury in Lunden acting as a brake on other indictments against judges and high-level officials, its verdicts served as an unofficial opener of the floodgates of charges against other defendants.

Apparently induced by the strength of the Government's case against them, Judge Sam Wilson and attorney Roger Flynn pled guilty to the charges against each of them. Peter Theos was spared the obligation to testify against Flynn in open court. Whether the outcome in the Lunden trial had any effect on either Wilson or Flynn to plead guilty was known only to them.

The actual Operation Greylord investigation resulted in the indictment of 92 people. Of those, 17 were judges, resulting in 15 convictions. Of the others, 48 were lawyers, 10 were deputy sheriffs, 8 were policemen, 8 were court officials, and 1 was a state legislator. The FBI hailed Operation Greylord as the most significant and successful undercover operation ever conducted.

As for the concern about lawyers for the Government lying to state court judges and losing their licenses to practice law as a consequence, the Seventh Circuit Court of Appeals wrote as follows in affirming the convictions in a real appeal of a judge convicted in Operation Greylord.

"The agents who made up and testified about the Operation Greylord 'cases' did so without criminal intent. They were decoys, and the Greylord cases made it easier to separate the honest judges from the dishonest ones. It may be necessary to offer bait to trap a criminal. Corrupt judges will take the bait, and honest ones will refuse....The phantom cases had no decent place in court. But it is no more decent to make up a phantom business deal and offer to bribe a member of Congress. In the pursuit of crime the Government is not confined to behavior suitable for the drawing room. It may use decoys, and provide the essential tools of the offense. The creation of opportunities for crime is nasty but necessary business. The FBI and the prosecutors behaved honorably in establishing and running Operation Greylord."

Although the opinion cited above was not directed to the State of Illinois commission with the power to regulate the conduct of licensed attorneys in the maintenance of their law licenses, the holding by the Court of Appeals cited above was both the first and last word in describing the honor with which the prosecutors and the FBI acted in Operation Greylord. The Court's opinion effectively ended their fear of the loss of licenses to practice in Illinois while investigating corruption in the state and local courts. No law license was ever challenged or threatened with revocation because of participation in Operation Greylord, and no undercover law enforcement agent ever faced a sanction for his or her conduct. ⚖

CHARLES P. KOCORAS
UNITED STATES DISTRICT JUDGE
NORTHERN DISTRICT OF ILLINOIS

Judge Charles P. Kocoras has been a United States District Judge in Chicago since 1980. He served as Chief Judge of the Court from 2002 to 2006. During his more than thirty years on the bench, Judge Kocoras has presided over thousands of cases in all areas of federal jurisdiction. He also served for six years as a member of the Criminal Law Committee of the Judicial Conference of the United States.

Before his appointment to the United States District Court, Judge Kocoras was a partner in the law firm of Stone McGuire Benjamin and Kocoras, where he concentrated his practice in the defense of federal criminal cases. Before that, Judge Kocoras served as Chairman of the Illinois Commerce Commission, a position which followed seven years of service as an Assistant United States Attorney in Chicago.

As Chairman of the Illinois Commerce Commission, Judge Kocoras and four other commissioners were responsible for the regulation of both privately owned utilities doing business in Illinois and intra-state motor carriers. As an Assistant United States Attorney, Judge Kocoras was personally involved in the prosecution of over two hundred criminal cases, with approximately twenty-five of those cases being tried to the court or jury. He also served in various supervisory positions including First Assistant United States Attorney to two United States Attorneys. Judge Kocoras was the recipient of a Department of Justice Special Commendation Award for Outstanding Service in 1974, and in 1976, he received the Department of Justice Director's award for Superior Performance as an Assistant United States Attorney.

Judge Kocoras attended night classes at DePaul University College of Law from 1965 to 1969 and graduated as valedictorian of his graduating class. He was an Adjunct Professor of Law at the John Marshall Law School from 1975 to 2015. In January 2011, he received the Award of Excellence as Adjunct Professor by the school. Judge Kocoras has also received the honorary Doctor of Laws degree from the John Marshall Law School and the honorary Doctor of Humane Letters degree from DePaul University. He was also the recipient of the Mary Heftel Hooton Award by the Women's Bar Association of Illinois in 2011.

Judge Kocoras served in the Illinois Army National Guard from 1961 to 1967. He was the Honor Graduate of the Radio School at Fort Knox, Kentucky, in 1961 and the recipient of the Chicago Tribune Award for Outstanding Guardsman in 1965.

Judge Kocoras has been on senior status since July 1, 2006. He wrote a book entitled *May It Please the Court* which was published in February 2015. The book was a story about Dan Webb, characterized as one of America's greatest trial lawyers. ⚖